"Let's Get Married," Taylor Said.

Carol stared at him, unable to reply.

"Don't you see," he continued, "it's what we have to do. I've been up for hours, thinking about everything, and it's the only solution."

Carol—sadly, slowly—shook her head.

Taylor looked stricken. "Don't you *want* to marry me?" he asked.

"Of course I do," she said quickly. "But I just want the reason for the wedding to be *me,* and how you feel about me. Not about your daughter…"

Dear Reader,

We all know that Valentine's Day is the most romantic holiday of the year. It's the day you show that special someone in your life—husband, fiancé...even your mom!—just how much you care by giving them special gifts of love.

And our special Valentine's gift to you is a book from a writer many of you have said is one of your favorites, Annette Broadrick. *Megan's Marriage* isn't just February's MAN OF THE MONTH, it's also the first book of Annette's brand-new DAUGHTERS OF TEXAS series. This passionate love story is just right for Valentine's Day.

February also marks the continuation of SONS AND LOVERS, a bold miniseries about three men who discover that love and family are the most important things in life. In *Reese: The Untamed* by Susan Connell, a dashing bachelor meets his match and begins to think that being married might be more pleasurable than he'd ever dreamed. The series continues in March with *Ridge: The Avenger* by Leanne Banks.

This month is completed with four more scintillating love stories: *Assignment: Marriage* by Jackie Merritt, *Daddy's Choice* by Doreen Owens Malek, *This Is My Child* by Lucy Gordon and *Husband Material* by Rita Rainville. Don't miss any of them!

So Happy Valentine's Day and Happy Reading!

Lucia Macro
Senior Editor

Please address questions and book requests to:
Silhouette Reader Service
U.S.: 3010 Walden Ave., P.O. Box 1325, Buffalo, NY 14269
Canadian: P.O. Box 609, Fort Erie, Ont. L2A 5X3

DOREEN
OWENS MALEK
DADDY'S CHOICE

SILHOUETTE *Desire*®
Published by Silhouette Books
America's Publisher of Contemporary Romance

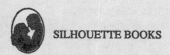

SILHOUETTE BOOKS

ISBN 0-373-05983-3

DADDY'S CHOICE

Copyright © 1996 by Doreen Owens Malek

This edition published by arrangement with Harlequin Books S.A.

® and ™ are trademarks of Harlequin Books S.A., used under license. Trademarks indicated with ® are registered in the United States Patent and Trademark Office, the Canadian Trade Marks Office and in other countries.

Printed in U.S.A.

DOREEN OWENS MALEK

is a former attorney who decided on her current career when she sold her fledgling novel to the first editor who read it. Since then, she has gained recognition for her writing, winning honors from *Romantic Times* magazine and the coveted Golden Medallion Award. She has traveled extensively throughout Europe, but it was in her home state of New Jersey that she met and married her college sweetheart. They now live in Pennsylvania.

One

Carol Lansing was dreaming, and the dream was very loud. The pounding noise went on and on, and it wrested her up from the depths of sleep. By the time she finally opened her eyes and tore the tangled sheets off her legs she realized that the pounding was actually hammering and it was coming from overhead, on the roof.

Carol pushed her hair out of her face as the room swam into focus around her. She was trying to remember the previous night, but she was still half asleep. Everything was dark; the drapes were drawn across the bedroom window. The sight of them made her recall, suddenly, when she had closed them and where she was. This was her father's beach house, the house he had left her after his death, and she was staying here for the summer to study for the upcoming bar exam.

The hammering, incredibly, seemed to be increasing in volume. Carol peered at the bedside clock and then closed her eyes again, sighing heavily. It was ten minutes after seven in the morning. At this ungodly hour some idiot was up on the roof making enough noise to rouse corpses that had been slumbering for centuries, not to mention an overworked law student who had just finished final exams five days earlier.

Carol swung her bare feet over the side of the bed and struggled into the robe she had left draped over a chair. She took one step and crashed full-force into a packing box on the floor. Muttering to herself, limping on her stubbed toe, she stumbled barefoot out to the living room.

The early morning sunlight blinded her and she stopped short, belting the robe around her waist and then shuffling over the pegged pine-board floor to the front door. The cottage consisted of a large parlor dominated by a fieldstone fireplace, with a kitchen and dining area to the back and two bedrooms off to the side. It was filled with cast-off rattan furniture and rag rugs, the remnants of her father's use and the debris of several tenants. Carol bypassed the second bedroom, putting her hands to her temples. The noise seemed to be surrounding her, as if she were inside a vibrating drum. By the time she reached the front of the house she was so angry that common sense had deserted her completely. She yanked open the door and confronted a startled workman, who stared back at her, metal tape measure in hand.

"What is going on here?" Carol demanded.

The workman took in her disheveled, recently-out-of-bed appearance, the bare feet, the carelessly knotted bathrobe tie. He said cautiously, "This house was supposed to be empty."

"Obviously it's not," Carol snapped, planting her hands on her hips.

They stared at one another.

"Would you mind telling me why you're creating such an infernal racket at a few minutes past dawn?" Carol inquired pointedly, raising her brows.

"We're renovating the house," the man said. "Putting on a new roof and aluminum siding, adding a covered deck."

"Oh, no, you're not," Carol said firmly. "I'm the new owner here, and I never authorized any improvements, so you can just run along, you and that cretin up on the roof."

The man held up his hand. "You'd better talk to the boss," he said.

"And who is that?" Carol asked, tapping her bare foot and lifting her chin pugnaciously.

The laborer pointed to the sky. "The cretin up on the roof," he said simply.

Carol swept off the porch and into the yard, her injured toe throbbing, lifting the hem of her robe as she walked. She was appalled to see two trucks in her driveway and several more workers employed there, moving equipment and shouldering boxes of tools. She turned abruptly and looked up at the shingled roof where a tall, slim figure was silhouetted against the early morning sun, kneeling and hammering, facing away from her.

Carol shaded her eyes and called loudly, "May I speak to you a moment, please?"

The hammering continued, uninterrupted.

Carol repeated her question. No response. Exasperated, she cupped her mouth with her hands and shouted at the top of her voice, "Hello!"

The man wheeled around and looked down at her, then set his hammer on the tar-paper shingles and got to his feet. She watched as he stepped nimbly across the sloping roof and then climbed over its edge. Carol drew in her breath as he hung, suspended by his fingers, and then dropped the remaining distance to the ground. He landed directly in front of her and she took a step back.

"Something I can do for you, miss?" he said mildly, folding his arms.

His action drew her attention to his body. He was wearing a short-sleeved, navy T-shirt that clung to his broad shoulders and slim torso. It exposed his arms, which were deeply tanned and well defined with long, ropy muscles. His faded jeans clung to his narrow hips, the heavy tool belt encircling his waist dragging the denim material low enough to expose the upper part of a flat, ridged abdomen. Carol raised her eyes slowly to see him examining her quizzically, the light blue eyes in his bronzed face direct and challenging.

She cleared her throat. "I'd like to know what you and your men are doing on my property," she said firmly.

"Renovating the house."

"I can see that. But it's *my* house and I never engaged anybody to do this work."

He shrugged and withdrew a folded piece of paper from his back pocket. "It's my guess that you're not George Lansing," he said dryly, opening the sheet and looking at it.

"I'm his daughter."

"Well, your father needs to work on his communication skills. I contracted with him to do this job on May 12. I was scheduled to begin today and have the job done by August 15." He handed Carol the paper and she saw that it was a cover letter for a contract with something called Kirkland Construction Company.

"My father is dead," Carol said flatly.

"I'm sorry to hear that, but the contract stands," the man said evenly, watching her. His thick blond hair had been bleached to the color of lemon peel from long hours in the sun and his face was so sun-browned that his eyes looked ethereally pale.

"What are you talking about? This is my house now and I don't want you here!" Carol said incredulously.

"If your father is dead, then his estate is responsible for his contracts."

"I *am* his estate and I'm telling you to go!" Carol said, her outrage building with every passing second.

The man held up his hands. "Don't get mad at me, lady, I'm just explaining the situation. I have a contract, I've begun the work, I expect to complete it and get paid for it at that time."

Carol tried to keep her temper in check. "Look, Mr...."

"Kirkland. Taylor Kirkland."

"Mr. Kirkland, I inherited this place when my father died suddenly of a heart attack at the end of May. He said nothing to me about renovating it, maybe he intended it as a surprise, but I don't even plan to keep this house, much less put out money to improve it. I was just going to spend the summer here studying for the bar exam and then put it on the market in the fall. I've sublet my apartment in New York, so you see I have no place to go for the next couple of months, and you're making far too much noise for me to be able to concentrate on anything. So if you will please clear your men out of here, I'll make sure you get paid for the day."

"Nope," he said shortly, and took the paper from her outstretched hand, stuffing it back into his jeans.

"What do you mean?" Carol demanded as he turned his back on her and headed for the house.

"I delayed other projects and hired extra men to do this job, and I'm going to finish it."

"But I don't want you to do the work!" Carol said to his back, enunciating very clearly, as if speaking to someone with impaired hearing.

"That's your problem." He climbed hand over hand up the front porch railing and then launched himself onto the roof with the grace of a puma scaling a mountain crag.

Carol simply couldn't believe it. "And what if I said I was calling the police?" she yelled up at him.

"Go ahead and call them. I'll just show Tom Delaney my contract and you're going to look pretty foolish." He picked up his hammer and began to pound the shingles again, effectively ending the conversation.

Carol glared up at him for a few enraged moments, stymied, then stalked back up the porch steps.

"You can tell your boss that I'm going to see my lawyer today," Carol said regally to the first workman, passing him as she went back into the house.

He waited until she had closed the door and then scrambled up to join the tall blond on the roof.

"What's going on, Tay?" he asked his boss. "That little lady is pretty upset."

"Mother Superior is trying to expel us, but we're staying," Tay said lightly.

"What?" the workman said, bewildered.

"I contracted with her old man and now that he's dead and she's inherited the place, she wants to cancel the deal."

"Can she?"

"Not without a hassle, Mike. The last time this happened to me, when old Hendrickson died, I won, and his kids had to let me finish the addition to his house. So I'm going to continue unless I get some legal papers that tell me I can't.''

Mike shrugged and walked off, delivering himself of a parting comment. ''Hey, Tay, you should schedule an eye exam as soon as possible.''

''What's that?'' Tay said, glancing up at him.

''If that stacked brunette looks like a nun to you, I think you need a pair of glasses.''

Tay smiled faintly and went back to nailing a shingle into place.

Carol returned to the bedroom, stripped off her nightclothes, and took a bracing shower. Then, still wrapped in a towel, she dialed her father's lawyer in Avalon and got his voice mail. She explained the situation and asked for him to call her back. Then she made coffee and tried to endure the din surrounding her, closing her eyes when something crashed from the roof to the ground outside the kitchen window. She retreated into the living room with her cup of coffee and waited for the phone to ring.

Contracts law was not her specialty, but her memory of the few courses she had taken made her fairly certain that she could force Kirkland to stop work. She was just annoyed that she would have to spend precious studying time getting rid of this intractable man and his crew of industrious noisemakers.

Carol sighed and took a sip of her drink. She had decided to spend the summer in Strathmere, a small New Jersey shore town, because it was quiet and out of the way, the perfect place to study. She had finished law school in May. Her father had seen her graduate and then died two weeks later, leaving her this house, where she had spent her childhood summers. Carol hadn't been back to the cottage in Strathmere since she was ten, when her mother had died. There had been too many memories in the house for either remaining Lansing to enjoy staying there, so her father had rented it out during the succeeding years. Carol had no idea why he had decided to renovate it; he had been dating someone during the last year of his life and maybe he had wanted to bring Gloria to the house. Carol herself had only decided to come to Strathmere after his death, when she had remembered the town's isolation and knew the house would be empty. She had felt that fifteen years was enough time to make the absence of her mother from the house less keenly felt, and she was right. Now only the good memories remained, and she had been looking forward to a quiet summer.

Strathmere was located between Ocean City and Avalon on a barrier island off New Jersey's coast. Between the island towns and the peninsula, which ended in Cape May, flowed the Intracoastal Waterway on the west and the Atlantic Ocean on the east. With its elderly clapboard houses, single main street, and dusty, unpaved alleys housing fishermen and boat mechanics, Strathmere was not a tourist attraction. It had no boardwalk or amusements like Sea Isle City or Avalon or Wildwood farther to the south. It was isolated, accessible by only one bridge and clinging to the northernmost tip of the strip island. It had one decidedly noncontinental restaurant/bar and a handful of permanent residents whose families had been living in the little town for generations. The abandoned schoolhouse just a few doors away from Carol's cottage was two hundred years old, built by laborers with their own hands; the streets leading away from the main drag to the water were little more than pebble-strewn footpaths, just wide enough to accommodate cars. Since its location discouraged "summer people," its population was low all year 'round, and it was the perfect place for Carol to hole up with her books and block out the rest of the world until the ordeal of the bar exam was behind her.

And now here she was in the midst of this sudden and infernal din, saddled with a raucous construction crew that refused to depart. That man Kirkland was certainly rude. She intended to make short work of him and his deafening little band.

The telephone rang. Carol went into the kitchen to answer it, avoiding the bedroom extension because of the noise right above that room.

"Hi, John," she said in response to the greeting from her father's lawyer, John Spencer.

"What seems to be the problem?" John asked.

"I described the problem on your voice mail," Carol replied crisply. "I have this construction crew at my house and I want to get rid of them. Whatever they're doing, I don't want them to do it, and the boss refuses to call them off and leave."

"Which company is it?" John asked. Carol heard the rustle of papers in the background as he took notes.

"Kirkland Construction."

"Tay Kirkland?" John asked in surprise.

"Yes. That's who he said he was, anyway."

"He's usually pretty reasonable."

Carol made a disgusted sound. "Not on this occasion, I'm afraid."

"Well, look. I don't know what's going on, your father never said anything to me about renovating the cottage, and if he signed a contract, he did so without my knowledge. I'll give Kirkland a call and see if I can resolve the situation."

"He's up on my roof, if you want to talk to him," Carol said dryly. "Do you want me to get him?"

"He's usually in his office after he lets his crew go at three," John said. "I'll talk to him then. If you want to stop by my place around five, I should have something for you."

"Fine," Carol said shortly. "I'll see you at five."

She hung up the phone and went to the kitchen window, gazing out at the driveway where Tay Kirkland was now standing at the mouth of his pickup truck, directing the action. The sun glinted off his blond hair and ignited the gold in his watch as he raised his arm to gesture to one of his men. Carol studied the scene for a few moments, then went back to her bedroom. She went though the clothes she had brought with her, choosing a blue sundress with a bolero jacket and a pair of sandals that would not put pressure on her injured toe.

She would curl up in here to study and try her best to block out the noise. It was only for one day. After that the problem would be solved.

The construction crew departed precisely at three, and Carol enjoyed an hour and a half of blissful silence before she got into her father's car to make the trip to Avalon. The weather was pleasant, with a sea breeze all the way, and she left the windows open for the salt air. Her good spirits had been restored by the time she reached John Spencer's office, which was housed in a converted Victorian summer home about two blocks from the beach. But her upbeat mood dispelled rapidly when she saw who was sitting inside the lawyer's suite, waiting for her.

"Tay came right over when I called him about your situation," John said to Carol, almost apologetically, correctly reading the expression on her face when she spotted his companion. "He brought the contract with him."

Kirkland rose to his feet as she entered the room and then sat again when she did.

The secretary, who was leaving for the day, pulled the office door shut behind them and then Carol heard the thud of the outer door closing, as well. She looked from one to the other of the two men slowly.

The silence echoed.

Taylor Kirkland was now wearing a dark blue, pin-striped suit of tropical wool, with a light blue shirt and a navy-and-white-figured tie. He sat with a manila folder in one tanned hand, the other resting lightly on the arm of his chair. Carol noticed that the blond hairs on his fingers were bleached almost white, and that his nails had recently been scrubbed scrupulously clean. The color of his shirt made his eyes look even more vivid than before, and his wavy hair had recently been wet combed into submission. It was now drying and curling around his ears and onto his forehead, lightening to a color millions of women regularly tried, and failed, to achieve in beauty salons.

Carol looked away from him deliberately.

John cleared his throat. "Well, I suppose we should get down to business," he said.

"By all means," Carol said.

"I've read Tay's contract and I must say that everything in it looks to be in order," John said. "Your father *did* contract for Tay's firm to do the work on the house and it was scheduled to begin today. Tay is within his rights to insist on completing the job."

Carol glared at him. "Even if I don't want the work done?" she asked.

John sighed. "He can insist on specific performance from the estate, Carol. You're not a layman, you know the rules."

"I can get an injunction to keep him off the property until this is resolved in court. That's in the rules, too."

"To what end?"

"To the end of peace and quiet," Carol said shortly.

John shook his head. "The court calendar is dead down here at the best of times—the fishermen don't sue each other and the tourists stick to Avalon. The case will come up in a week and Tay will be back working on the house in ten days."

"I take it you think I'd lose?" Carol inquired darkly.

"I think there's a good chance of it."

"So I let Kirkland here finish a job I don't want done and for which I don't have the money, or he sues *me* for interference with the performance of his contract and holds me up for a year on selling the house," Carol said succinctly.

John pressed his lips together in silence. They both knew that was about the size of it.

"Thanks a lot, Kirkland," Carol said sarcastically, and rose to go.

Kirkland, who up to this point had said nothing at all, rose abruptly and put his hand on her arm. Carol started and pulled back as if he had burned her. She looked up at him, riveted by the intensity of his gaze.

"I'm not trying to take advantage of you," he said quietly. "I've hired extra men, cleared my schedule of other contracts, and invested a bundle in the materials for your job," he said. "If I'm forced to stop it now, I won't be able to unload the materials or get back the business I turned away. If you'll just let me finish the job, I'll take payment in the form of a builder's lien against the property and you can pay me once you sell it. John says cottages like that one, so close to the water, go in a matter of weeks down at that end of the street. And you'll get a lot more for it once it's fixed up and modernized.''

''I see that you two boys have already figured this all out for me,'' Carol said pointedly, folding her arms.

''It's not like that,'' Kirkland said softly.

''How is it?''

He closed his eyes briefly, then opened them again. ''I know you're a lawyer...''

''Not quite yet, Mr. Kirkland, and it looks like your busy little troop of hammering devils just may keep me from ever becoming one.''

''Look, Miss Lansing. I really don't want to give you a hard time. Can't we reach some sort of compromise?''

His tone was low, almost seductive, and Carol realized that, without seeming to, he was charming her.

''Like what?'' she said warily.

''I could adjust my schedule and work from eight to four so you could sleep an hour later in the morning every day,'' he said reasonably.

''And the noise?'' she asked archly.

He sighed. ''I could use electric staple guns instead of hammers, pad the windows and doors while we're there, to muffle the sound, and do the noisiest roofing at the end of the day when it won't be as disturbing to you,'' he replied.

Carol glanced at John, whose expression said, *He's trying, isn't he?*

Carol looked back at Kirkland, who was waiting tensely, his tall frame motionless.

''All right!'' Carol said, throwing up her hands.

John grinned, and Kirkland permitted himself a half smile, his light eyes warming just a little.

"Why do I feel that I've just been outgunned?" Carol said wearily.

"Not ungunned," John said. "Merely enlightened. You'll make a tidy profit on the house once it's renovated, even with the costs of the work deducted."

"John, I understand that," Carol said, holding up her hand. "But my concern at the moment is having a quiet place to study during the summer, not becoming a real estate profiteer."

"I'll do everything I can to help you study," Kirkland said evenly, and Carol looked at him again.

It seemed that he meant it.

Carol nodded resignedly.

"Can you two shake on it?" John said genially, obviously relieved that he wouldn't have to take legal steps to resolve their differences.

Kirkland extended his hand, and Carol reached out to grasp it. His palm was callused and work-hardened, but large and warm. Her fingers disappeared into it and then he relaxed his grip. She snatched her hand back hastily.

There was an awkward silence, then John said briskly, "Well, I'm glad we were able to come to terms on this. Now, if you don't mind, I'd like to get home—my wife will probably carve me up with the roast."

Kirkland shook hands with John, glanced once more at Carol and said, "I'll be back at your house at 8:00 a.m. tomorrow, then," and left.

John packed his briefcase as he said, "Wait just a moment, Carol, I'll walk out with you."

Carol paused as he punched a button on his phone and then picked up his keys. She walked beside him as they left his office and he stopped to lock his door before proceeding down the steps that led to the street.

"How are you getting along, Carol?" John said. "You must miss your dad."

"I do, but I've been so busy I don't think his absence has really sunk in yet. Since I was away at school I really didn't see him much, just talked to him on the phone."

"Ever hear from Gloria?" John asked warily.

Carol shook her head. "She's afraid that I'm going to contest the bequests to her in my father's will, but I don't plan to do that. She can keep whatever he gave her as long as I never have to see her again."

"No love lost there, I take it."

Carol shrugged. "When I saw that she was depositing my father's money in a bank account with her name on it, I was not favorably impressed."

John nodded. "I think that's why he never told me about his renovation of the cottage. He was afraid I would attempt to talk him out of it."

"Why?"

John glanced at her nervously.

"Tell me," Carol said levelly.

John shrugged. "I think he planned to give the place to Gloria once it was redone. He just happened to die before he changed the provision in his will that left the cottage to you."

Carol was silent.

"I'm sorry," John said gently, "but I thought you should know in case she comes sniffing around, offering up witnesses to testify about his intent to give it to her."

"Are there any?"

John shrugged. "Who knows? But I don't think she'll get anywhere. Any judge in the world would determine that she has already been well compensated for her period of 'companionship.' If she does file a complaint I don't think it's likely to get past a preliminary hearing. I just wanted you to be prepared for the possibility.''

Carol nodded. She wasn't worried about Gloria; all Gloria wanted was money, and so more money would make her go away. Carol was much more concerned about passing the bar exam.

They had reached John's car, a green BMW sports car, and as he unlocked it he said, ''Why don't you come home with me and join us for dinner? Beth would love to see you.''

''Thanks, John, but I'd like to get back to Strathmere. I still have unpacking to do and I want to be ready to hit the books early tomorrow.''

''Okay, but you have to give me a rain check.''

''I will.''

John tossed his briefcase onto the passenger seat of his car and slid under the wheel. As he started the car Carol said suddenly, ''John, what do you know about this Taylor Kirkland?''

The older man squinted up at her as he adjusted his seat belt. ''Why do you ask?''

''Well, he's going to be on my property every day all summer, isn't he?'' she replied obliquely.

John thought a moment. ''He's a local boy, quiet, minds his own business. He built that construction company up all by himself from what I hear. His father was a fisherman. I don't know many other personal details, but in business Kirkland has a reputation for being quite fair and aboveboard. That's why I was surprised when he gave you trouble.''

''I guess he's just determined to follow through on the contract my father signed,'' Carol said glumly.

''You can't blame Kirkland for that.''

"But I'd really like to," Carol said, grinning, and they both laughed.

"Sure you won't take me up on that offer of dinner?" John asked, glancing at his watch.

Carol realized that she was detaining him. "No, go ahead. And thanks for your help."

"Call me if you need anything else," John said, and shut his car door. Carol stepped back as he glided out of his parking space and then pulled out of the lot.

Carol walked toward her father's car—his used backup model; Gloria hadn't come after it because she was doubtless more satisfied with the new foreign sports sedan she had received. Carol was just getting into the driver's seat, warm from sitting in the late afternoon sun, when a wave of dizziness came over her. She had to lean forward with her head on her crossed arms, hands gripping the steering wheel for support.

How long had it been since she'd eaten? She realized with alarm that supper the night before had been her most recent meal. She'd been in such a snit over her unwanted visitors all day that she'd forgotten about food.

The dizziness passed and she lifted her head. She knew from experience that she couldn't drive back safely unless she had something to eat, and John's car was now out of sight. She glanced across the street at a restaurant she'd been in with her father several times. Like John's office, it was housed in a restored Victorian-style home. The first-floor rooms of the old house had been converted into a large dining salon. Usually the place required reservations but she was probably early enough on a weeknight to just walk in and be seated. She stood gingerly, then relocked her car and went across the street.

She was right. The dining room was only half full and she was given a secluded table near the back. She had just picked up the menu when a masculine voice next to her said, "Are you following me?"

Two

Carol turned abruptly and saw Tay Kirkland standing at her elbow. His tie was off, his jacket over his arm, and his open collar exposed a matte expanse of brown throat. When she looked startled at his remark, he smiled slightly and she realized that he was joking.

"I thought you'd be taking off with John," he added.

"No, he was going home and I didn't want to intrude. But I started to feel a little shaky when I got into my car and thought I'd better come over here for dinner."

"Didn't eat today?" he asked.

She shook her head.

"Too upset about the big bad construction crew invading your domain?" he asked archly.

Carol gazed at him in exasperation. "You may think my concern is ridiculous, Mr. Kirkland, but if you've ever tried to study with hammering and drilling surrounding you in stereophonic sound, you would know that it's not.''

''Please call me Tay. And I've never been big on studying, but I can imagine that the kind of noise my outfit makes doesn't exactly aid concentration.''

Carol said nothing. It was nice of him to be understanding now that he was getting what he wanted.

''I'd like to explain myself better than I did in John's office if you'll give me a chance. Do you mind if I join you for a minute?'' he asked.

Carol hesitated, and he saw it.

''Never mind,'' he said quietly, and turned to go.

Before she knew what she was doing, Carol had leaned forward and placed her hand on his wrist. He froze and looked down at her inquiringly.

''Please stay,'' she said, then regretted her impulse when his eyes locked with hers, searching and very blue. His candid examination made her feel coltish, uncertain, and she was relieved when he pulled out a chair for himself at her table.

''Okay to sit?'' he asked.

She nodded.

He settled in across from her and folded his arms in front of him. With his height and broad shoulders he dominated the small round table as if he were sitting in a child's playhouse.

''I wanted to explain to you why I took such a hard line with your contract,'' he said.

''I think you already did that.''

''Not completely. When I first started this business ten years ago, I got burned by quite a few people who backed out of their deals after I had ordered all the materials and hired the men for the jobs.''

"So you've said," Carol observed impatiently. Why was he cornering her like this just to repeat himself?

He shook his head, holding up his hand. "Let me finish, there's more. I have to think about my future business. In my industry, if you get a reputation for caving in when the client changes his mind, you're in trouble. You have all sorts of people ordering up work and then backing out when they decide to pay for their daughter's shotgun wedding or Junior's braces or a trip to the Bahamas instead."

"I didn't order the work. My father did."

"I understand that, but from my perspective it's the same thing. I have to enforce my contracts or the accumulated costs, over time, will drive me out of business. I'm growing, but I'm not that big a company yet and I can't afford to absorb the losses the way a national outfit could. It's simple economics."

Carol said nothing.

"Do you see my point at all?" he asked wearily, a slight note of pleading in his voice making her look at him more closely.

"Do business with a national outfit?" she suggested, and he grinned, breaking the tension.

"They like to enforce their contracts, too, and they can afford to hire people like you to make sure they do."

"Nobody's going to be hiring me unless I pass the bar," Carol muttered.

"You will."

She glanced at him, one eyebrow arched. "You're a soothsayer?"

"I recognize determination when I see it," he replied. "I'd hate to be one of the bar examiners if they turn you down."

Carol smiled.

"So are we okay? No snits, no pouts, no grudges?"

"I never pout," she said.

"I don't imagine you do. An Uzi would be more your style."

"You make me sound quite formidable, Mr. Kirkland."

"I asked you to call me Tay."

"All right, Tay. No snits and no pouts, I promise."

He nodded. "Good."

Carol studied him as he sat across from her. Was it possible he was really concerned that she would be angry with him? Or was he merely worried that she might interfere further with his renovations if he didn't placate her now?

"I'll do a great job and your place will be worth a fortune when I'm finished," he added, and Carol had to smile again.

Kirkland might be quiet, as John had said, but she had to be careful of the man facing her across the snowy restaurant tablecloth.

He was just too attractive to have on the premises every day.

As if reading her thoughts, Kirkland pushed back his chair and stood.

"I guess I'll be going," he said.

"Would you like to stay and join me?" Carol asked, and she felt him measuring her expression, as if deciding whether her invitation was motivated by mere politeness.

"I hate to eat alone," she added, and that seemed to make the decision for him.

"All right," he said, and sat again, dropping his jacket on the chair next to him.

"Have you been here before?" Carol asked.

He nodded.

"What's good?"

"The clam chowder is excellent, seafood's the specialty. The swordfish and the trout almondine are usually top-notch."

He sounded like a man who spent a lot of time in restaurants.

The waiter, who had been watching them during their earlier conversation, seemed relieved that Carol's companion had decided to stay and materialized at Tay's side.

"Are you ready to order?" he asked.

Tay looked at Carol. "I haven't given you much of a chance to look at the menu," he said.

"That's all right, I'll take your suggestion," Carol replied. She turned to the waiter and said, "A bowl of the clam chowder and the grilled swordfish, please."

He nodded, scribbling. "White or red chowder?" he said.

Carol looked at Tay.

"Red," he advised. "And I'll have the same. With the baby vegetables and a bottle of the house chablis."

The waiter disappeared and Tay selected a breadstick from the basket on the table.

"Do you often forget to eat all day?" he asked Carol, biting into the stick, which snapped under the assault of his teeth.

"Not often. It's a bad idea when you have low blood sugar. Everything tends to get a little hazy around the edges."

"I could never forget to eat," he said, smiling. "My stomach always reminds me."

"It happens only when I get really preoccupied. I passed out during exams once, right after civil procedure. The instructor was mortified, he thought I had fainted because I was afraid I'd failed the test. I had to tell him that I'd been studying so hard I'd skipped breakfast and lunch.''

''I guess I should be flattered that I'm as much of a distraction as a civil procedure exam,'' Tay said lazily.

Carol met his eyes, then looked away.

''What is civil procedure, anyway?''

''Torture. Sheer, maddening torture. It's all confusing cases and decisions about who can bring a case, where it should be brought, if it has enough merit to be heard, on and on and on. It's the Waterloo of the first year of law school and everybody dreads it.''

''I'll bet you got an A,'' he said, polishing off his breadstick.

Carol glanced at him, startled.

''Did you?'' he said.

She sighed. ''Yes.''

He chuckled, the low, throaty sound drifting across the table toward her as the waiter brought their appetizers.

Carol picked up her spoon and Tay watched her reaction as she tasted the soup.

''Very good,'' she said.

''Not too spicy?''

''No, it's fine.''

They ate in silence for a while, and when Carol's bowl was almost empty he said, ''Feeling better?''

''Much.''

''I think you need someone to take care of you,'' he said quietly.

''I'm doing just fine,'' Carol replied firmly. ''Lots of people skip meals, it doesn't mean they need a keeper.''

He let that pass, pouring them both a glass of wine when the waiter brought the bottle.

"I hope you like this, it's actually much better than some of the big label stuff," he said, saluting her with the glass.

Carol sipped hers obediently and nodded.

"Did you spend all your summers down here when you were a kid?" Tay asked, watching her.

"From the time my father bought the house, yes."

"I don't remember you," he said, as if he should.

"A few years is an unbridgeable gulf between kids," Carol replied.

"But not between adults," he observed.

The busboy cleared the table and shortly afterward the waiter brought the main course. Tay speared a tiny carrot with a tine of his fork and said, "How do they get these things so small? Are they shrunken or something?"

"Beats me. They must grow that way, like Bonsai trees. The fish is delicious."

"I'm glad you like it. Maybe this experience will encourage you to eat regularly. I can't have you passing out on the sidewalk in front of my construction crew."

"I shouldn't have told you that story," Carol muttered, and he chuckled.

Carol stared at him, riveted in spite of herself, then took another sip of her wine.

"Do you like living at the seashore all year 'round?" she asked.

"Sure. Why not?"

"Well, I should think it might be dismal in the winter—gray ocean, gray skies, empty beaches."

"Spoken like a true summer person," he said dryly. "Actually, the beach in winter is very nice."

"If you're an Eskimo."

"If you like peace and quiet, as you supposedly do."

Carol paused with her fork halfway to her mouth. He had scored a point off her without even trying.

"I only meant that the image of a deserted and wind-swept beach is a lonely one," Carol said quietly.

"For landscape artists, maybe. But I like the isolation, it helps me to think. When the tourists flood in over the Memorial Day weekend I always want to head for the hills. At least Strathmere is off the beaten path, I could never stand living in one of the big towns that turn into a Mardi Gras every summer."

"Don't like the Ferris wheels and coin toss booths, eh?"

"I avoid all amusement parks," he said. "Have you ever noticed that people do things on vacation they would never do at home?"

"You mean toting around the boardwalk souvenirs, the funny hats and the giant blue teddy bears?" Carol asked.

"And who are the merrymakers? Drunken teenagers in wrecked cars and middle-aged tire salesmen in hula skirts," he said.

Carol giggled. "You don't paint a very pretty picture of the summer visitors. I was one of them, you know."

"I'm sure you weren't one of the worst. You had a home here and stayed the whole season. The worst of them blow in for a week or two, stay soused the entire time, then leave a trail of litter behind on the beach and a trail of beer cans on the way out of town."

The waiter approached and said, "Is everything all right?"

"You can take this, I'm done," Carol said.

"Do you want anything else?" Tay asked.

"No, I'm fine."

"Coffee, dessert?" the waiter said.

"Just coffee for me," Carol replied.

Tay nodded in agreement. Carol felt as if she were on a date, with Tay directing the action, even though their meeting had been a coincidence.

"Do you like what you do?" Carol asked as Tay picked up the bottle and tipped it to top off her glass.

Carol covered it. "I have to drive," she said.

He replaced the bottle in its stand. "Construction?" he said.

"Yes."

He nodded. "I like working with my hands, and it's very satisfying to see the completed job and know I was responsible for it. I can drive up any street in Strathmere and see how my efforts have improved or redone the old houses, in some cases even saved them from collapsing."

"I see."

"Do you feel that way about the law?"

She hesitated before answering. "The law is malleable. It can be a force for good, but it can also be used in negative ways."

"I guess that means you have to be careful."

"Yes, it does. You have to be careful about what type of law you practice and which cases you choose."

Their coffee came, and they sipped it as Tay asked, "Does that mean you won't be representing any Mafia dons?"

Carol smiled. "It seems unlikely."

"Embezzling bankers?"

"They can usually afford the experienced, high-priced practitioners. That's not me."

"Deserting husbands, deadbeat dads, Wall Street tax evaders?" he suggested.

"I can see you have the same impression of lawyers as you do of summer visitors," Carol said, laughing.

He shrugged. "Your profession hasn't been getting very good press for a long time."

"That's true, but it doesn't mean all lawyers are creeps."

"You certainly don't look like a creep," he said mildly.

Carol glanced toward the entrance of the dining room and saw that a line had formed there. She also noticed that the waiter was hovering anxiously.

"I really have enjoyed this, Tay, but I have to go," Carol said, putting down her cup. "Could you call for the check and then—"

"The check is mine," he said, interrupting her firmly. "I'll see you out to your car."

He settled the bill and they left the restaurant, the soft evening air embracing them as they emerged into it.

"Nice night," Tay observed, taking Carol's arm to guide her across the street.

"I have always loved a summer dusk," Carol replied. "Of course, it does take some of the sparkle out of it when you consider that more car accidents occur at this time of day than any other."

Tay laughed; when she looked at him he was shaking his head.

"That's the sort of thing a lawyer would know," he said.

"Or an insurance adjuster. It's something about the change in perspective, drivers have difficulty dealing with the diminishing daylight. It's actually safer to drive in full dark."

"I'll bear it in mind, Ralph Nader," he said.

They reached her car and he waited while she unlocked it and got in, starting the motor and turning on the lights.

"Thanks for letting me join you for dinner," he said quietly.

"Thanks for the dinner."

"Good night."

"Good night." Carol watched him walk out of the lot, saw the way his bright hair caught the light from the street lamp, noted the flexing of his muscles as he shouldered briskly into his coat. She finally dragged her eyes away.

She almost wished she had not had dinner with him. He wasn't just her nemesis anymore, he was a person now, a person with a sense of humor and a point of view.

And a very distracting presence.

What she didn't need now, she thought again as she started her car, was a distraction.

And Taylor Kirkland promised to be a powerful one.

Tay unlocked the door of his truck, realized that he was wearing his jacket again, and took it off to toss it in the back. As he inserted the key into the ignition he thought about the new summer resident on Schoolhouse Lane in Strathmere.

Carol Lansing was an unexpected and problematic development.

He liked her already; he liked her too much, and he was concerned that his compromise with her would slow his work schedule. But it was either make the deal or have her tie him up in the courts. Or raise Cain every time one of his workmen dropped a hammer. His infallible charm routine didn't seem to work too well on her, either; at dinner she had seemed to be as smart and aware as she was pretty. He only hoped she'd stay inside the house and study, as she'd said. The last thing he needed was a curvaceous brunette in a bikini parading past his men while they were trying to work.

And while he was trying to work.

He was already having difficulty putting her out of his mind.

He turned the key in the ignition and gunned the motor.

Carol was up, showered and dressed when Kirkland Construction descended on her the next morning. As she waited for her friend Jane, who had gone to law school with her and lived nearby in Stone Harbor, to arrive for a study session, the crew muffled the windows and sealed the doors before they set to work. The effect was peculiar: instead of loud and insistent pounding filling the house, the noise now sounded like distant thunder. Carol tried to ignore it and assembled her note cards and books on the kitchen table, rising to let Jane into the house when her knock came at the front door.

"What is going on here?" Jane said breathlessly as she entered the cottage and looked around wonderingly. "Are you experimenting with plutonium? This place is sealed off like a murder scene."

"It's a long story," Carol replied wearily.

"Well, you'd better tell me, I'm just bursting with curiosity," Jane said as she dumped her backpack on a chair.

Carol related the dismal tale as she poured a cup of coffee for her friend.

"And is that towering creature with the wavy blond hair the villain of this piece?" Jane asked archly. "He nodded to me as I breezed past him, laden with my twenty pounds of books. He took them from me in silence and deposited them on the porch, then nodded again when I thanked him."

"That's the one. John Spencer says he doesn't talk very much."

"For heaven's sake, Carol, who cares if he can talk? That's the most gorgeous man I have ever seen! I can't believe you were trying to get rid of him, I would have been begging him to stay."

"I must be a little more interested in passing the bar than you are, Jane," Carol said dryly.

"Oh, come on, the noise isn't that bad."

"Today it isn't that bad. Yesterday it sounded like the anvil chorus was being performed on my roof."

"So you had a romantic dinner with him?" Jane asked, selecting the most interesting tidbit from Carol's previous recitation.

"I did *not* have a romantic dinner with him," Carol replied in a strong voice. "We shared a meal because we both happened to be in the same place at the same time. The whole event lasted little more than an hour."

"How could you let that opportunity pass? You should have nailed his feet to the floor for the night!"

"I was angry with him, Jane," Carol said, beginning to get annoyed with her friend, too. "He was insisting on completing a job I didn't want done. Don't you get the picture?"

"I'll bet you weren't angry by the time dinner was over," Jane observed slyly.

Carol shot her a look.

"So he's staying?" Jane said, cutting to the chase.

"Obviously."

"Well, at least I'll have the scenery to look forward to around here, since you're a complete grouch."

Carol lifted a stack of three-by-five index cards and placed them on the table between them.

"May we begin with these notes on contracts?" she said, changing the subject to the work at hand.

Jane reached for them resignedly and began to read out loud.

Around noon Jane suddenly raised her head and said, "What's that sound?"

"Blessed silence. The crew is taking a lunch break."

Jane leapt up from the table and walked over to the front window, peering past a wad of padding to look out at the front lawn. "Oh, be still my heart! Blondie is taking off his shirt."

Carol scrambled over to the window and yanked the shade down to the sill.

"Why did you do that?" Jane demanded, outraged.

"Do you want him to see you peering out at him like some swooning teenager?"

"Anyone is permitted to look out the window, Carol. You're being ridiculous."

The phone started ringing, sparing Carol a reply. When she answered it she heard a sweetly feminine voice say, "Hi, this is Madeline, Mr. Kirkland's personal assistant. Would it be possible for me to speak to him? I have to consult him about a business matter."

Carol put the caller on hold and headed for the door.

"Where are you going?" Jane demanded.

"The call is for Kirkland," Carol said shortly. Before Jane could answer, Carol was out the door and down the steps, striding across the lawn, which was now covered with a layer of fine dust and large wood chips. Kirkland looked up from his sandwich as Carol stopped in front of him.

"Help you?" he said.

"There's a call for you inside the house," Carol said.

He rose immediately, untying his T-shirt from his waist and slipping it over his head. He left the sandwich behind on the tailgate of his truck where he had been sitting. His men watched as he followed Carol back into the house.

"Over there," Carol said, pointing to the phone sitting on the kitchen table. Both women left the room as he leaned against the wall and spoke into the receiver, the call box under his arm.

"I'll bet it was a woman," Jane muttered under her breath as she and Carol entered the living room.

"She said it was a business matter," Carol whispered back.

"Huh. Monkey business."

"Jane . . ."

"He put his shirt back on to come in here. Very gallant."

Carol opened her mouth to reply, then thought better of it as Kirkland joined them.

"Thanks," he said to Carol.

She nodded. His attitude toward her was distant and businesslike; it was as if their shared dinner had never happened.

"The mobile phone in my truck has been on the blink for the last couple of days. All I get is static. But I've got them working on it, you won't be bothered again," he added.

"It was no bother," Carol said.

"Hi, I'm Jane Langley. How do you do?" Jane said, stepping forward and sticking out her hand.

Kirkland shook it, glancing once at Carol and then back at Jane. "How are you?" he said to her.

"Great. Seems like you guys are making a lot of progress on the house," she said brightly.

He nodded.

"Construction must be an interesting business," Jane observed.

"It has its moments," he replied shortly.

"Do you work mostly in the summer?" Jane asked, emitting a flood of pheromones.

"Outdoor jobs. In the cold weather I do plastering and flooring, that kind of thing." He looked once more at Carol. "Well, I'd better get back out there. Thanks again." He walked out of the house, and the front door closed behind him moments later.

"'Construction must be an interesting business,'" Carol chirped, batting her lashes, imitating Jane. "About as interesting as watching grass grow. Really, Jane, sometimes you can be embarrassing."

"At least I talked to him. You stood there like a floor lamp."

"Perhaps I'm reluctant to make a fool of myself," Carol said.

"Fine, Carol. You can play it cool if you like. I'm a human being even if you're not, and I plan to try again."

"Then you're not studying here with me. I am not going to have you panting after him every time you come to this house." Carol turned her back on Jane to pour herself a cup of coffee.

"You're forbidding me to talk to him?"

"Don't be ridiculous."

"Then what? I can ask him out?"

"Don't you think that's a bit forward?"

"Don't you think you're a bit Victorian?"

"Oh, for heaven's sake, Jane, what are we arguing about? The man is probably married." Carol put the pot back on the warmer and picked up her cup.

"He's not married."

Carol whirled to face her, the cup in her hand sloshing liquid. "How do you know?"

Jane burst out laughing and leveled an accusing finger at her friend. "You *are* interested in him, I *knew* it!"

"I'm interested in him, okay?" Carol said quietly. "You're right. It's utterly absurd. The man undoubtedly hates me because I tried to get him thrown off this job, but there's just something about him . . ."

"There certainly is, and I must say I'm relieved that you've noticed it. At school you were so glued to your books I wondered if you were preparing for a somewhat unusual legal career in a convent."

Carol sighed. "Jane, this conversation is getting us nowhere. I am starving and I'm going to make lunch. You may join me if you like, if you can stop talking long enough to chew."

Jane pulled out a chair at the kitchen table and sat. "I have one last thing to say."

Carol closed her eyes. "As long as it is the last thing."

"Now that you've met someone you want, go after him."

"In my own way, Jane. Not yours."

Jane held up her hands to indicate innocence. "I'll be a fly on the wall," she said meekly.

"That'll be the day. Tuna, grilled cheese, or turkey?"

"Tuna," Jane replied glumly, and hooked her sandaled feet in the rungs of the chair.

Three

Two weeks went by, during which the roof was reshingled, the new back deck took shape, and Jane arrived to study every day. Tay Kirkland came and went like clockwork, directing his men, talking to Carol only when it was necessary, interrupting her routine as little as possible.

It was exactly what she had requested, but she didn't like it. She longed for an interlude of personal intimacy like their meal in Avalon, some indication that he knew she was alive, but he stayed out of her way. She caught glimpses of him, but the most she received in response to her greetings was a nod. Jane constantly urged Carol to go outside and talk to Tay, but she couldn't strike up a conversation with all of his employees looking on like a studio audience.

Maybe Jane could, but Carol couldn't.

One day when Jane had decided to spend the morning at the law library in Cape May, researching a point of the New Jersey criminal code, Carol noticed that Kirkland arrived alone. She watched as he left his truck and disappeared around the corner of the house. Curious, she opened the door to the back deck and found him crouched on the ground, filling a crack in the foundation with what looked like grout.

He glanced up as she emerged.

"What are you doing?" she asked, leaning over the railing to get a better look.

"Sealing the cellar wall. We disturbed the ground and caused a few fissures in the stone. If I don't fill them with this stuff, water will seep in and cause problems in the future."

"Where are the guys?"

"They're finishing up another project on the west side of town. This is a one-man job anyway." He looked over her shoulder. "Where's your buddy?"

"She went to look something up in the Jersey archives. The procedure for bringing cases into court varies from state to state and we have to bone up on the local methods."

He nodded one of his frustrating, noncommittal nods. Carol mustered her courage and said quickly, "Would you like to come in for a cup of coffee?"

He looked up from his work and studied her with such intensity that Carol grew uncomfortable. Was this a major decision? Had she asked him to marry her?

"Sure," he finally said shortly, putting down his grout gun. He rose in one smooth motion and took a rag from his back pocket, wiping the gray gunk from his fingers as he came up the steps. He paused on the landing next to Carol, looking down at her. She was tall, but he was taller. It was an unusual sensation for Carol to look so far up into a man's eyes.

"Come in," she said hastily to break the spell. When she opened the door he put his arm above her head to hold it for her, and she caught a brief scent of soap and sun-warmed male flesh. Then he moved and the moment passed.

"Have a seat," she added.

He pulled out a chair and dropped into it, easing down onto the base of his spine and stretching his long legs in front of him. Today he was wearing an aqua T-shirt, faded from many washings, which dyed his eyes the color of a Bermuda inlet at dawn. He watched her move around the kitchen, pouring coffee, setting out a plate of cookies, and she fancied she could feel his eyes boring into her back. When she sat across from him he took a bite of one of the cookies and said, "Good." He smiled. "She cooks, too."

"Not really. They're from a mix."

"Well, you didn't burn them."

"True." She watched the working of his throat as he swallowed. "How long do you think it will take to wrap up this job?" she asked.

"Still trying to get rid of me?" he countered.

Carol looked at him directly. "No."

He shrugged. "It's hard to say. A lot of variables are involved—the efficiency of the crew, the quality of the materials, the weather..."

"The weather? It's been nice every day."

"Hurricane season is coming soon, and this house is in a bad spot."

"Why?"

"The locals call this inlet Hurricane Bay. The close headlands on either side of it create a funnel that narrows to a point just past your place. It makes a wind tunnel in a storm. The schoolhouse roof has blown off several times in the last ten years."

"I didn't know that. We never had any trouble when I came here as a kid."

"The weather pattern has shifted. A friend of mine is a meteorologist at a radio station in Atlantic City and he's been tracking it."

"I see." Their eyes met, and Carol knew that neither one of them was thinking about the weather.

He held the ensuing silence for a long beat and then asked, "You doing anything for lunch?"

"Peanut butter and jam?" Carol suggested.

He grinned. "I'm not fond of peanut butter myself. I think I ate too much of it as a kid. Would you like to go out and get something?"

"Where?"

"The only restaurant in town is Cater's, and it doesn't open until three," he said, laughing. "We'd have to drive to Avalon."

"Why don't we stay here? I could make lunch, if you'd like to join me."

"Don't go to any special trouble."

"It's no trouble."

He rose, draining his mug. "Is twelve-thirty okay?" he said, setting the cup back on the table.

"Twelve-thirty is fine."

"See you then." He sauntered across the kitchen and out the back door, letting the screen door slam behind him.

Carol smiled to herself and began to clear the table.

The morning progressed with glacial speed; Carol kept glancing at the clock, only to discover that just a few minutes had passed. She finally gave up trying to study. She prowled the house, straightening things that didn't need moving, shuffling books on the shelves, watering the plants she'd brought from her apartment, listening for Tay's movements outside. At twelve o'clock she made the salad and sliced the strawberries for dessert. At twelve-twenty she heard the gush of the lawn hose and looked out the window to see Tay stripped to the waist, washing under its stream.

Carol stood to the side and watched as he let the water cascade over his hair and torso. There was a ring of sunburn around his neck and his whole upper body was a golden brown, his arms below the biceps several shades darker. Carol studied the movement of the muscles framing his spine as he thrust his free hand through his damp hair, then she looked away as he turned off the tap and hung up the hose. She ran to the mirror and fluffed her hair, checking her lipstick and looking up with a smile as he tapped on the door.

"Hungry?" she said.

"You bet." He'd put on another shirt he must have had in the truck, a yellow polo that highlighted his water-darkened blond hair and contrasted with his tan.

He seemed to look wonderful in everything.

"Can I help?" he asked as she set the table.

"No, everything is done."

"Looks good," he said, sinking into the chair she indicated. Carol put a glass of iced tea in front of him and then sat across from him as he lifted a fork and dug into the salad. She waited for his reaction. He looked up and saw her watching him.

"Great," he pronounced. "What is it?"

"*Salade niçoise.*"

"From a mix?" he said, and she laughed.

"No, that's my own concoction."

"And this?" he asked, gesturing to his other plate.

"Cold chicken. Doesn't it look familiar?"

"Oh, I just wondered if there was anything fancy going on there. I liked to be warned."

"Lemon glaze."

"Well, that doesn't sound dangerous." He chewed reflectively for a few moments and then added, "My wife used to make elaborate dishes, things I never heard of. Always tasted good, though. Except this one time she must have overreached herself, she tried some sort of fish in a baked crust and it fell in, looked like a smashed custard pie." He smiled, remembering.

"You were married?" Carol said cautiously.

He nodded, wiping his mouth with a napkin.

"Divorced?" she asked.

"No, she was killed in a car accident five years ago."

Carol was silent for several seconds and then said, "I'm terribly sorry."

"Thanks."

"Any children?"

He put down his fork. "A girl," he said quietly. "She's seven now, almost eight. She's not with me."

The tone of his voice warned Carol not to ask any further questions on that particular subject. An uncomfortable silence prevailed until Carol said brightly, "Jane and I have been getting a lot of studying done."

He looked up at her, taking a sip of iced tea. "Think you'll be ready to take the bar when the test comes up?"

"I hope so," she said. "I'm trying, but the amount of information to cover is overwhelming, I feel like I'll never remember it all."

"What's it like to go to college for so long?" he asked. "I went to work right after high school."

"Oh, in some ways it's an escape from real life, but I'm going to have to face that very soon."

"Do you think you'll like practicing law?"

"I like the internship I'm doing at a firm in New York. I'm thinking about continuing with family law now that I have some experience with it."

"Here?" he asked.

"Maybe. I plan to take the New Jersey bar first, then the state section of New York's, so I'll be licensed to practice in both places."

"You're not eating," Tay observed, pointing to her full plate.

"I guess I wasn't very hungry."

"You made all of this just for me, didn't you?" he said.

"No, I..." She met his eyes and shrugged. "I guess I would have settled for the sandwich if I were alone."

"I appreciate it. Lunch usually isn't like this. I'm a big patron of convenience stores."

"You never eat at home?"

"Rarely."

"Why?"

"No inclination, no time. The business keeps me pretty busy. Speaking of which, I'd better get back out there."

"I have dessert."

He grinned. "You've sold me."

Carol took the plates from the refrigerator and gave him his portion. He dug in with relish as she made coffee. He paused once to ask, "What's in this?"

"Fruit, yogurt, some granola and crushed nuts, brown sugar, honey."

"I'll probably fall asleep after this meal," he commented. "If you spot me through the window unconscious on the lawn, just come outside and kick me."

Carol smiled and began to clear the table as he added, "I really didn't expect you to fix anything special."

"I appreciate the company," she said, stacking plates.

"You have company every day," he said slyly.

"Yes, but you're not asking me to name the five most common torts contested in courts," she said, putting the dishes in the sink.

"I promise I will never do that," he replied solemnly.

"Good." She handed him a cup of coffee and then resumed her seat across from him.

"What's a tort?"

"Please, don't remind me. It's a legal term for a non criminal infraction, and there are a million of them."

"Sounds like an Italian dessert."

"I wish they were so I didn't have to stay up until the wee hours reading about them. They're studied during the first year and by now I've forgotten everything I ever knew. It's like a blank slate up there, *tabula rasa.*"

"Sounds like a typical case of exam panic to me," he said.

"It's some kind of panic, and it will eventually give way to hysteria and then finally progress to screaming dementia."

He made a muffled choking sound and she glanced at him over the rim of her cup. He was trying not to laugh, but his grin was roguish.

"It isn't funny."

"I'm sure it's not," he said, sobering.

"Long years of work are riding on this test, and if you flunk it three times you can't take it again."

"You will pass on the first try."

"You've said that before. You have influence with the board of bar examiners?" Carol inquired.

"I have influence in several bars," he replied helpfully, swallowing coffee.

"I don't think that will do it."

He put down his cup and scraped the last of his dessert out of the dish.

"This has been great," he said, rising. "But I really have to get back to work."

"Okay."

"If I don't finish what I had planned for today it will throw off my schedule and I'm running a little late as it is."

"Go ahead, Tay. I'm not keeping you," Carol replied gently, studying his expression.

He stood looking down at her sheepishly, flushing slightly. "That's not what I meant. I feel like I'm just bolting this food and running out the door."

"You could stay and sing a few songs if you like. Do you know 'Home on the Range'?"

He smiled, shaking his head, then glanced away from her. "I guess I'm surprised that you're being so nice about all of this. You have reason to keep your distance."

"Your crew's presence isn't the burden I thought it would be."

"No?" he said, looking back at her.

"No."

"What about my presence?" he asked softly.

A horn sounded in the driveway next to the house, causing them both to jump.

"I guess that's Mike. I asked him to bring over some supplies," Tay said. "Well, thanks for the lunch and..."

Carol waited.

"I'll see you later," he concluded lamely.

Carol watched him walk across the room in his long-legged stride and go out the door. Then she went to the sink to rinse the dishes.

She wanted to throw the plates on the floor and run after him, but a lifetime of restraint and cautious behavior held her back from following her instincts.

What would she do when the summer ended and she never saw him again?

"So you had lunch with him today?" Jane asked, munching one of the cookies Carol had made. Dusk was gathering beyond the kitchen windows and they had just closed the books following a long afternoon of studying.

"Yes."

"That's progress, isn't it?"

"I don't know if you could call it that. We were just here by ourselves and it seemed logical to eat together."

"I wonder if that was an accident," Jane mused. "His showing up alone when I wasn't here, I mean."

"You're assuming he has psychic powers?"

"Well, it does seem odd, doesn't it?" She lifted her shoulders.

"It was a random coincidence, Jane. They happen all the time."

"Did you find out anything interesting?"

"He doesn't volunteer much personal information and I couldn't interrogate him. He did mention that he was married, but his wife was killed in an accident and he doesn't have custody of his child."

Jane stared at her. "That's quite a bit. I wonder who has custody of the kid."

Carol shrugged.

"There was probably something sordid in the case, otherwise the child would be with him. Custody usually goes to the surviving parent unless there's hanky-panky involved."

"Hanky-panky?" Carol said, raising one eyebrow.

"You know what I mean. Maybe he had a girlfriend before the wife was killed."

"Maybe you have a vivid imagination." Carol glanced at the clock on the wall and said, "My God, it's after eight. I thought I heard my stomach rumbling. I wonder if there's any tuna left."

Jane moaned. "No more tuna, please, I'm growing gills. Can't we get an honest-to-God hamburger some-place?"

"Cater's is nearby, but if memory serves me, the regulars are rowdy and the food is just marginal."

"It couldn't be any worse than what we've been eating for the last week," Jane said gloomily.

"Thanks."

"If I grow eight inches and wear a blond wig will you make *salade niçoise* and lemon chicken for me?" Jane asked innocently.

Carol threw an eraser at her.

"Come on," Jane said, slipping her bare feet into her sandals and picking up her handbag. "I'm sick of the rule against perpetuities and I'm sick of these four walls. Let's get something to eat and take the evening off, what do you say?"

"All right, but it's Friday night. Cater's will be packed."

"I can stand it."

"Just let me comb my hair and I'll be right with you," Carol said, going into the bedroom. She glanced at her-self in the mirror over the dresser and sighed, then opened the top drawer and took out a navy tank top that was slightly less faded than the one she was wearing. She pulled it over her head after discarding her old one and tucked it into her jeans, then rummaged in the drawer for her lipstick. She applied it and then ran a comb through her dark hair, tucking it behind her ears.

She was ready.

"Let's go," she said to Jane as she emerged, and they headed together for the front door.

Cater's was a short walk of several blocks, near the entrance to the main causeway. Once they were outside the sea air surrounded them like a warm bath, smelling of salt and the burgeoning tide.

"No matter how hot it is during the day, there's always an evening breeze," Carol said as it caressed her hair. "I remember that from my summers here years ago."

"I'm still glad we have the air conditioner in the kitchen," Jane replied. "The afternoons would be broiling without it."

"Imagine what it's like to work outside all day."

"But Tay and his guys all have great tans from it. Which reminds me, I'm going to get to the beach soon if it kills me," Jane muttered as they walked down the lane. "I'm the only person in this town with skin like a bedsheet."

"What about me?"

"You're not a person, you're a computer. It seems lost on you that plenty of people are paying to stay nearby and sample the sun and surf. You've always got your nose to the grindstone like a gerbil on a treadmill."

"I'll swim when I've passed the bar."

The sun was setting in a blaze of orange and purple streamers as they climbed the wooden steps to Cater's.

The restaurant was a rambling, barnlike structure. Its name was written in pink neon across the shingled roof and it was surrounded on all sides by a gray, weather-beaten deck. The door opened into a noisy, smoke-filled bar, which fed into a dining room fronting the inlet at the back. There was a line at the entrance to the dining room, so they gave their names and retreated to the bar, where the crush of jabbering humanity and the jukebox music combined to produce instant deafness.

"Nice place," Jane screamed. "Did you bring your hearing aid?"

"I think it's a little quieter in there," Carol yelled, pointing to a smaller room with a dance floor on their left. They sidled over to it and sat at a tiny table, where they were joined immediately by a bartender in a checked apron.

"Ladies?" he said, grinning down at them.

"Two beers, any kind," Jane said.

He nodded and left as Carol said, "I don't want a beer, Jane. I don't like beer."

"I'll drink yours." Jane looked around as "My Boyfriend's Back" began to boom through the PA system connected to the other room. The dance floor filled quickly and Jane said suddenly in a hushed, melodramatic tone, "Uh-oh."

"What?" Carol asked, turning toward her.

"Look who's here."

Carol followed the direction of her friend's gaze and saw Tay Kirkland staring at her.

Four

Carol froze, then looked away from him quickly. When she glanced back he was doing a brisk version of a sixties' stomp with a slender redhead.

"Let's get out of here, Jane," Carol said, pushing back her chair immediately.

"What are you taking about?" Jane demanded, outraged. "I'm starving!"

"We'll take my car and go to Avalon."

"I'll be dead of malnutrition by the time we get there. I'm staying."

"Jane, for heaven's sake, this is totally humiliating. He's on a date and we're sitting here like the Bobbsey twins."

"The Bobbsey twins were a boy and a girl."

"Don't argue with me, Jane. I want to leave before he comes over here!"

"Too late now," Jane replied.

Carol closed her eyes and when she opened them Tay and his companion were standing next to her chair.

"Hi," Tay said. He was wearing tan chinos with a white oxford shirt and a cream V-neck sweater. His companion was wearing an expensive-looking pantsuit and a dazzling smile.

"Hello," Carol replied, and then sat through a numbing round of introductions and small talk before Tay and his friend finally moved to a nearby table.

"Well," Jane said briskly as Tay walked away, "Madeline's hairdresser needs to touch up her roots."

"That's his personal assistant," Carol said miserably, staring straight ahead.

"Is that what they're calling it these days?" Jane asked dryly, rolling her eyes.

"When he took the phone call at my house, the woman calling him was named Madeline. She said that she was his personal assistant."

"I don't like her shoes," Jane said, narrowing her eyes as Tay and Madeline stepped onto the dance floor again. Frankie Vallee's falsetto version of "Stay" filled the room, and Carol watched as they swayed and dipped to the slower music, with Tay lowering Madeline so close to the floor that her long hair swept the dusty boards.

"At least we know he can dance," Jane observed as the bartender brought their drinks.

"I'm going to wait outside the dining room," Carol said, rising. Jane trailed after her, carrying both mugs.

"Will you slow down? You bolted out of there like your jeans were on fire."

"Shut up, Jane, I'm not finding this amusing," Carol said tightly.

"Hey, hey, calm down a minute here. What are you getting all upset about?"

"Upset? Who's upset? I come here, bleary-eyed after studying all day and wearing an outfit left over from my college track team, to find Tay romancing a ravishing redhead modeling a *Vogue* ensemble. I can't imagine why I might be upset."

"You must really have a lech for this guy, Carol. I've never seen you like this," Jane said as the hostess motioned for them to come into the dining room.

Carol felt better once she couldn't see Tay any longer, but her appetite was gone. She fidgeted while Jane ordered. Finally she stood, saying, "I'm going to the ladies' room."

"Where is it?"

"Through the bar, as I recall."

"Good luck."

Carol pried her way through the crowd, hoping for a few moments of peace once she reached the inner sanctum. Her hopes were dashed, however, as a huge paw clamped down on her shoulder as she passed through the main room.

"Lucy!" chortled a huge, red-faced bear of a man in a plaid shirt. He had a bristling ginger mustache and a full pitcher of beer clasped in his other hand. "Ah nevah thought ah'd see you here."

"I'm not Lucy," Carol replied, trying to shrug free of him. It was a hopeless task. She almost threw her spine out of alignment but his grip never loosened.

"Ah missed you so much, darlin', ah was jes askin' Rudy t'other day, 'I wonder what became of mah li'l Lucy,'" he said, looming over her and breathing beer fumes into her face.

Carol looked around longingly for someone to help her with this overbearing drunk, but she saw only a sea of strangers. If there was a bouncer, he was nowhere nearby, and the man was inching closer while his heavy mitt on Carol's shoulder kept her immobilized.

"Aren't yah glad t'see me?" he asked. "How about a li'l kiss for Smoky, for ol' times sake?"

Carol's eyes moved to the pitcher as Smoky bent toward her. With the strength of desperation and the element of surprise she managed to grab hold of it and tip it, drenching her tormenter and herself with beer in the process.

Smoky gasped in shock, loosening his grip for a second, and Carol lunged away from him, her hair and shirt dripping beer. The crowd parted like magic, several of those nearby dodging out of the way and dusting their clothes for spots. Carol dashed blindly for daylight, skidding on beer suds, with Smoky in hot pursuit, his mean little eyes even meaner and littler with porcine rage.

Suddenly Tay appeared from the crush of people, grabbing Carol's arm and shoving her behind him, then stepping directly into Smoky's path.

The huge man stopped short, staring fixedly at Tay, who presented a slightly more formidable target than an intimidated woman.

"Get lost, Valentino," Tay said evenly.

"But...but...I know tha' li'l girl..." Smoky said, trying clumsily to sidestep Tay.

Tay moved with him. "You're too plastered to know anything, pal. Go dry off and leave the lady alone. She's with me."

Smoky looked around at his audience, then back at Tay. Evidently deciding that he didn't want to risk defeat in front of such a crowd, he shrugged and turned back to the bar, reaching out a hand for the bartender's proferred towel and mopping his hair.

Tay turned back to Carol, who was standing with her arms wrapped around her torso like a freezing swimmer, and clasped her hand.

"Come with me," he said, shouldering his way through the staring crowd. Carol kept her head down and followed him through the bar and out a side door, where he stopped in an alley and turned to face her.

"You okay?" he said.

Carol nodded shakily, thumbing her tangled, damp hair out of her eyes.

"I'm sorry I didn't get there sooner."

"Lucky for me you got there at all."

"It wasn't luck. I followed you."

Carol looked up at him.

"Why?" she asked softly.

"You seemed upset when I saw you inside. I wanted to know what was wrong."

"Nothing was wrong." A cool breeze drifted in from the water and Carol shivered in her damp shirt.

"Why don't you take that off?" Tay asked.

Carol stared at him.

He pulled his sweater off over his head and handed it to her, the woven cotton still warm from his body.

"The ladies' room is just inside that door," he said, pointing to a red Exit sign. "You'll feel better once you're dry."

"And smelling a little less like the brew that made Milwaukee famous," Carol added.

He smiled. "I'll wait for you here."

Carol slipped inside to a stall and took off her top and bra, donning Tay's oversized sweater. She rolled up the sleeves and let the hem fall to her hips. Then she emerged and combed her hair in front of the fly-spotted mirror, turning to go just as Jane barged through the door.

"Here you are!" Jane said. "What happened to you?" She stopped short. "And what are you wearing?"

"Tay Kirkland's sweater."

Jane's mouth fell open comically.

"Tay rescued me from a drunk in the bar," Carol said wearily, stuffing her damp clothes into her capacious purse. "I'll tell you all about it later. Right now I just want to go home."

"What about my food? I already ordered."

"Stay and have dinner. I'm capable of walking four blocks by myself."

"Are you sure? You look a little rocky."

"I'm all right. The guy bothering me was a bit large. And loud. But I'm over it."

"Thanks to Sir Galahad."

"Speaking of Tay, I left him outside. I should go back there and tell him I'm going home."

"Okay, Carol. I'll give you a call over the weekend. And good luck."

"Good luck?" Carol said.

"With Tay." Jane winked broadly and vanished into the hall. Carol followed, turning in the opposite direction to go through the exit.

Tay was leaning against the outside wall, his hands in his pockets, his shirt sleeves rolled to the elbows to expose his tanned forearms. His eyes looked very large in the parking lot's lights, which bathed them in a neon glow now that darkness had fallen.

"Feeling better?" he said.

Carol nodded.

"Do you want me to take you home?" Tay asked.

"What about your date?"

"My date? Oh, you mean Madeline? I'll go in and explain to her, she'll understand. She's with some other friends, she probably hasn't even missed me."

Carol held up her hand. "I can't ask you to do that. I'll walk home. I'll be fine."

"Are you sure?"

"Of course. Nothing happened, Tay, except that I overreacted. I probably could have gotten away from him without drowning us both in beer. What was he going to try, after all? We were in the middle of a crowd."

"You did the right thing. That guy's a disease. I've seen him in here before, you can't mistake that hair or that accent. He's always hitting on somebody."

"Well, thanks again, and good night." Carol walked away from the restaurant, and only permitted herself one glance over her shoulder as she turned toward the street.

Tay was standing exactly where she had left him, looking after her, his expression unreadable.

Carol took a shower when she got back to the house, washing her hair three times to eradicate the lingering, yeasty smell of beer. Then she bundled herself into a summer nightgown and robe and watched an old movie on TV, trying to put the events of the evening out of her mind.

She didn't want to remember her hairy friend from the bar, or Madeline, who looked as if she had had a vested interest in Tay long before Carol arrived on the scene. The whole episode had depressed her; she couldn't dismiss the feeling that she had made a fool of herself in front of Tay. She was just about to turn off the television as the news came on when her doorbell rang.

Was it Jane returning? Carol couldn't imagine who else it might be at this late hour. She switched on the porch light and through the half-glass door saw Tay standing on the porch, dressed as she had last seen him, his hands jammed into his pockets.

Carol's heart began to beat faster as she belted her robe and pulled open the door. Tay straightened, his eyes seeking hers soberly, his expression tentative.

"Hi," he said.

"Hi."

"I just wanted to come by and check on you. I wasn't happy with leaving you to go off by yourself after that incident in Cater's tonight."

"I'm fine, Tay. Where's Madeline?"

"I dropped her off before I drove here," he replied. "May I come in?"

"Of course." Carol stepped aside, feeling like an idiot for letting him stand on the entrance mat like a traveling salesman.

He came into the living room, looking around as if he had never seen it before that moment. When his eyes returned to Carol's face he said quietly, "I don't know what I'm doing here."

Carol was silent.

"I just had to come."

She nodded, afraid to speak.

"Did you get all of that beer out of your hair?" he said, reaching out to touch a lock that lay against her shoulder.

"I think so. Some women rinse their hair with brew after they wash it. Beer supposedly makes it shine."

"You don't need any help in that direction."

"I could never do it anyway. Who wants a head that smells like a keg party?"

He smiled.

"I'll wash your sweater and return it to you tomorrow."

"Don't worry about it."

"No, no, I want to do it. After all, it was kind of you to lend it to me and you should get it back clean. It looks new and I'm sure you'll need it." Carol knew that she was babbling and was powerless to stop talking. She heard her voice running on, as if from a distance, and barely restrained herself from clamping her hand over her own mouth.

"I wanted to kill that overgrown brute when I saw him put his hands on you," Tay said.

"I told you, it was nothing."

"I think I was really just jealous," Tay added huskily, his eyes locked with hers.

"Jealous?" Carol whispered, afraid to breathe.

He nodded solemnly. "I have wanted to touch you so badly myself."

Carol closed her eyes. She could feel her control waning; she was not going to be able to resist this approach. When she opened them again, Tay was inches away; he saw the look on her face and swept her into his arms.

He felt even bigger than she had anticipated, and lean, his waist reed-slim under her hands. She tilted her face up for his kiss as his mouth sought hers, and she heard his soft sound of satisfaction when their lips met. The embrace escalated quickly with a fierceness that consumed them both; it seemed they had waited so long. They were like kids in their wondering discovery of each other.

Carol clung to him helplessly, aware of his every sound, every movement. His mouth was soft, pliant; his arms, by contrast, like steel bands as he pressed her to him. Carol had imagined kissing him so many times that the reality was almost miraculous. She felt his hands

running down her back, the warm sensation of skin on
skin as his lips moved to her cheek, the shell of her ear,
her neck. He pushed her robe off her shoulders and she
felt it puddle at her feet as his supple fingers dug into her
bare flesh, the thin silk of her gown a slight barrier to his
seeking hands. She gasped as he bent her over his arm
and his mouth left a trail of kisses down her throat and
into the vee of her bodice. The straps slipped, exposing
the tops of her breasts. He kissed them voraciously, his
face flushed and hot, burning her skin as he slipped an
arm under her knees and lifted her into his arms, sitting
on the sofa with her in his lap.

Carol twined her arms around his neck, heedless of
anything but the moment. He smelled wonderful, like
piney soap and the long days he spent in the sun, and she
buried her lips in his thick hair as he mouthed her
through the gossamer cloth, teasing her nipples into hard
peaks. He ran one hand up the smooth expanse of her
bare leg, shifting her weight so that she lay partially under him, his body pinning hers. Carol moaned when she
felt his full arousal. She pulled his shirt loose from his
jeans and caressed the satiny surface of his back and
shoulders, slipping her fingers under his belt as he
gasped, the tension in his body gathering and coiling under her hands. She turned toward him when he lifted his
head to kiss her again, more deeply than before, and she
felt the hardness of his teeth against her tongue.

Carol was lost, all her inhibitions fleeing in the wake
of a desire more intense than anything she had ever felt
before. She found herself tugging Tay's shirt from his
pants, trying to undress him as he kissed her repeatedly,
as if he could never get enough of her mouth. When her
seeking fingers found his flat nipples nested in soft hair,
he moaned and lay back, letting her caress him until he

couldn't stand it any longer. He seized her, pushing her gown down to her waist and taking one swollen nipple into his mouth, laving it until it was drenched and swollen. Carol whimpered with pleasure, tangling her fingers in his hair and holding his head against her.

"Love me, Tay," she whispered, willing to beg. "Please love me."

As if the sound of her voice had broken a spell, Tay sat up suddenly and pulled back, his expression anguished.

"I can't do this," he muttered hoarsely, running one trembling hand through his disordered hair. "I'm sorry, Carol, I shouldn't have come here."

Carol stared up at him in confusion, her clothes in disarray, too stunned to speak.

"I'm sorry," he said again. "I can't explain. I know I've misled you terribly, please forgive me." He set her aside and got up, stuffing his shirt back into his pants.

Carol stared after him in total disbelief, then fell back on the sofa as the door shut behind him.

She didn't move as the hot tears began to seep from under her lids.

He was gone, as if she had imagined him.

Tay drove aimlessly over to the bridge and then got on the highway headed for Avalon. He didn't know or care where he was going, he just had to keep moving. He was too wound up to sleep, and the car seemed to drive itself as the traffic flowed around him in a steady stream.

Why had he gone to Carol's house? He had done irreparable damage by leading her on and then bolting. He knew that, but he hadn't been able to stay away. For the past couple of weeks, every moment he didn't see her, he was thinking about her. And something about the way she'd looked after she'd dodged that drunk in Cater's had touched him so deeply that he hadn't been able to rest until he saw her again. She was always so brisk, so capable, that the thought of her in a vulnerable position, even for a moment, had made him face what he had been feeling for her since the beginning.

But he couldn't feel that for anybody, much less act on it, and now she probably hated him.

He couldn't blame her if she did. She had shown him how much she reciprocated his need, and he had flung that revelation back in her face.

Tay was at a loss; he literally didn't know what he was doing. It had been so long since he'd felt that irresistible pull, the overpowering longing that mastered everything else. Not since Alice. And his feelings for Carol Lansing might prevent him from ever regaining custody of Alicia.

He had to resist Carol. There was no choice about it.

His face a mask of pain, he turned the car around and headed back toward Strathmere.

Five

Carol spent the rest of the weekend in a state of shock. She couldn't imagine why Tay had shown up at her door and deliberately seduced her, only to take off just when she was at the point of submitting. Was it the payback for her initial reaction to his presence on her property? Then why had he been so nice since, at her house recently, and at Cater's? It was maddening and upsetting, all the more so because Carol was as choosy as Jane had said. She'd had only two previous intimate relationships, both of which she had ended. Being summarily rejected when she was so attracted to a man was a new and devastating experience.

She couldn't bear to think of facing Tay again.

As it turned out, that was the least of her problems. From the moment Tay showed up to work on Monday morning, he ignored her. Aside from the short nods she received when she passed him on the walk, she might as

well have been invisible. Faced with the impenetrable wall
of his silence, Carol's shame and discomfort gradually
turned to anger. On Wednesday at noon she walked over
to Tay in full view of his crew and handed him his laun-
dered and folded sweater.

"I wanted to give this back to you," she said evenly. "I
thought Madeline might be able to use it."

Tay's neck flushed a dull red but he didn't say a word.
He took the sweater and tossed it carelessly onto the
passenger seat of his truck.

Carol stalked back into the house, where Jane was
waiting for her.

"Are you ever going to tell me what's up between you
and Sir Galahad?" Jane asked.

"Nothing's up. Can't you tell?"

"I mean, what happened? Last I heard he rescued you
from some geek at Cater's, which I thought was a prom-
ising development, but now the atmosphere between you
has icicles forming on the end of my nose. Are you going to let me in on the cause of the deep freeze?"

"I don't want to talk about it."

"Obviously not. But you'd better do something because your concentration has not exactly been improved
by your tiff with Blondie. I didn't think anything could
disturb your fixation with passing the bar exam, but this
standoff certainly has."

Carol walked past the kitchen table and looked out the
back window, where she saw Tay's men just breaking for
lunch. She watched Tay walk up the drive and speak to
one of them, noticing the longish wavy hair clinging to
the back of Tay's neck and the hip-shot stride she would
already know anywhere.

She looked back at Jane and said in a low tone, "He
came here Friday night after I got home."

"With Madeline?" Jane asked incredulously.

"No, he dropped her off first."

"That was decent of him. What did he want?"

"To see if I was all right. At least, that's what he said when he arrived, but it was like we didn't have to talk, we both knew..."

"Oh, boy. That explains a lot. You went to bed with him?"

"Of course not," Carol replied, coloring.

"I didn't think so, Carol, unless you had a personality transplant when I wasn't looking."

"But I came close," Carol said. "I've never felt that way before in my life. He touched me and everything else just went right out of my head." She sighed. "And now he won't even talk to me."

"Why?"

"It's a mystery. Just when we were getting close, he jumped up and said he couldn't do it, or he had to go, or some other lame excuse. I forget exactly. I think I've blocked it. But he dashed out Friday night and ever since he's been treating me like I'm carrying typhoid."

"It sounds like he's confused," Jane said.

"*He's* confused! What about me? I didn't run after him, he came here! I'd like to smack him."

"Smacking him is not what you'd like to do."

"All right, all right, I still want him—that hasn't changed. But the question is, what now? I can't just act as if nothing happened."

"That's what he seems to be doing."

"Yes."

"And that puts your little nose out of joint," Jane said archly.

"I know you find this humorous, Jane, but I'm perfectly serious. I may not have a lot of experience in this area, but I know he didn't leave because he suddenly stopped wanting me. It was more like he had fought with himself to come to me in the first place, and then remembered the battle at a crucial moment."

"Then what do you think is happening? Madeline?"

"He can't care about Madeline or he wouldn't have gone from her to me in the same night."

"He could if he's a womanizing jerk."

"I don't think he's a jerk. It's something else."

"Then take the initiative," Jane said. "Go up to him and ask him what the hell is going on."

"I can't do that. He kissed me once, Jane."

"From your description it sounds like your encounter involved a lot more than a kiss."

"That still doesn't imply a lifetime commitment. I can hardly call him on the carpet and demand to know his future intentions."

"All right, it's your decision. But it seems like doing nothing is driving you crazy." Jane paused thoughtfully. "Are you sure his wife is dead?"

"That's what he said."

"Men say a lot of things."

"What are you implying? That he has a crazy wife chained in his attic like Mr. Rochester?"

"It wouldn't hurt to ask a few questions in town."

Carol fixed Jane with a gimlet stare. "Jane, if you start running around Strathmere interrogating people about him, I swear I will poison your diet soda."

"I'll be discreet."

"Don't do it at all. I mean it."

Some sort of power tool started whirring outside and Jane said wearily, "Sounds like somebody took a short lunch."

Carol sat across from her and said, "We might as well get started on the Uniform Commercial Code. We don't have much time left before the test."

Jane checked her watch. "I'm going home at three," she reminded Carol.

Carol nodded.

"And don't worry about Tay Kirkland," Jane said. "Something tells me he'll be back for more."

Carol didn't answer.

She wasn't so sure.

The workmen departed after Jane left and the house became very quiet. Carol was walking past the window on her way to the sink when she saw Tay's truck still in the driveway. She stopped and looked out; she could see him in the driver's seat, talking on the mobile phone. She glanced at the clock. What was he doing still sitting in the cab of the pickup over an hour after his men had gone? She watched him a moment longer and saw him fold his arms on the steering wheel and then rest his head on them.

Something was wrong.

Carol headed for the door. He might not want to see her but he was going to, right now.

Carol was standing next to the truck door before Tay even realized she was there.

"Tay," she said softly.

He looked up, and she saw that there were beads of sweat standing on his forehead.

"What is it?" she said, concerned. "What's wrong?"

He looked trapped, completely miserable. "I threw my back out," he said, staring straight ahead. "I left last and everybody was gone by the time I realized I couldn't drive. I've been sitting here trying to raise somebody on the phone.''

"Why didn't you call me? I was thirty feet away!"

He looked at her, then away. "I didn't think you would want to talk to me."

Carol sighed, shelving that discussion in view of the current crisis. "Can you move over on the seat? I'll drive you to the hospital.''

"No."

"No? Do you plan to sit frozen behind the wheel for the rest of your life?''

"I'll be able to drive in a minute."

"By your own admission you've been unable to drive for quite a few minutes."

" 'By my own admission'?'' he said, closing his eyes. "You really are a lawyer, aren't you?''

"Yes, I really am. Now stop being so obstinate and let me help you.''

Tay sighed resignedly. "Can you drive a stick shift?'' he asked.

"Yes, I can. You're pale beneath your tan and obviously in pain. Move over.''

He bent his head and gingerly inched over on the seat, the effort obviously costing him a great deal. A fresh sheen of perspiration broke out on his upper lip.

"How did you do this?'' Carol asked, jumping up next to him in the cab.

"I wrenched my back playing football in high school, and every now and then it acts up again. I can go for a long time with no problem and then suddenly if I happen to move just the wrong way...''

"Agony,'' Carol supplied.

He said nothing, but he didn't have to agree with her. What he was feeling was plain on his face.

"Tay, you're so foolish," Carol said softly. "Did you really think I wouldn't want to help you?"

He looked out the window on the passenger side of the truck and said nothing.

Carol drove Tay to the emergency room at Avalon General. The entire trip was conducted in silence; Tay never spoke and Carol didn't question him. When they arrived at the hospital Carol watched as two attendants helped Tay onto a gurney and wheeled him inside. She stood at his side in the waiting room as he gave his information to the admitting office and was fitted for a plastic bracelet. She learned that he was thirty-two and was allergic to penicillin. When he was about to be wheeled through the double doors to the examining room he caught at her hand and said from his prone position, "Thanks for bringing me in. I'll be fine now. Goodbye."

"I'll wait for you."

"You don't have to do that...." he began, but his voice was swallowed up as he was whisked through swinging doors and into the next room.

Carol sat in a plastic chair in the anteroom and looked around at the vending machines, the piles of tattered magazines, and the office of the triage nurse, which faced her. There were two other patients waiting for treatment: a teenager with an ugly cut on his leg and a toddler with a high fever. The teen sat sullenly staring at the floor and the baby babbled deliriously in his mother's arms as she dabbed at his face with an ice pack. Carol picked up a magazine and read an article on acupuncture while the wall clock on her left ticked audibly. The toddler had been called into the other room and forty minutes had passed before Tay emerged, leaning on the arm of an attendant.

"How do you feel?" Carol asked anxiously, rising as they approached her.

"Better. They gave me a muscle relaxant and a prescription for pain pills. I can get home okay, I'll call a cab."

"Don't be ridiculous, Tay, the truck is right outside. I'll get it and pull it up to the door."

Tay's resigned expression indicated that he knew further argument would be useless. By the time he was installed in the passenger seat he had accepted the situation. He gave the directions to his place in a monotone, then subsided into renewed silence for the duration of the drive home. As they finally turned into the street he had indicated, Carol realized that he lived above the storage garage for his business. There was an exterior flight of stairs leading to a door on the second floor.

"Do you think you can make those stairs?" Carol asked doubtfully.

"I can make them," he replied firmly.

The muscle relaxant had enabled him to walk, albeit unsteadily, so they climbed the flight slowly, with Tay leaning heavily on Carol's arm.

"I hate this," he said suddenly, his tone vehement, grinding his teeth as they paused midway up the stairs.

"What?"

"I hate having you see me like this," he clarified, panting audibly.

Carol said nothing.

"I don't know why you're helping me, anyway," he added, not looking at her.

"I wasn't going to leave you stranded in your truck, Tay," Carol replied.

They stopped in front of the door as he pulled out his keys. Carol looked up at him, his profile outlined against the late afternoon sun.

Carol knew she couldn't press him about his past behavior; the man was barely able to stand on his feet. She went with him through the immaculate, stainless-steel-applianced kitchen and into a living room that featured an oversized sofa, several reclining chairs, and walls lined with loaded bookshelves.

"The bedroom is that way," he said, pointing to a rear hall. Carol felt him depending on her assistance as they headed for it; his fatigue was palpable. After all, he had worked a full day of heavy labor and had then battled severe pain for several hours. When she eased him toward the bed, Tay dropped onto it gratefully and closed his eyes. Carol took off his work boots and lifted his legs onto the spread. He sighed deeply.

"You just rest there," Carol said. "I'll go and fill the prescription."

His eyes shot open. "Go home. You've done enough. I can last till morning."

"That shot is going to wear off, Tay, and when it does you'll need these pills. The pharmacy's only a few minutes away. I'll be back in half an hour."

He sighed again and then propped himself up on an elbow, reaching into his back pocket for his insurance card.

"Take this," he said. He gave her the card and some money, then collapsed back onto the pillows.

"Okay. I'll be right back. Get some rest while I'm gone, if you can."

His eyes were already closing again. Carol tiptoed out of the Spartan bedroom, which featured little more than a king-size bed, a dresser and a set of weights, then closed the door behind her. She was back in the truck and at the pharmacy within a matter of minutes. When she returned to Tay's apartment with the medicine, he was fast asleep.

Carol stood with the bag in her hand and looked at the clock. If she just left the pills and went home, the chances were that he would sleep through the time to take them and then wake up in agony. And no matter how he had treated her recently, she didn't feel right about just leaving someone in his condition to weather such a situation completely alone.

She went back into the living room to get a book, and was struck by the sterile quality of the walls, the side tables. There were no pictures or mementos of any kind, not even a snapshot of the child he had mentioned. The layout resembled that of a sample home, as if no one lived there. And from what she had seen of Tay, he really didn't live there; he was always working.

Before settling down to read, she glanced back into the bedroom. Tay had changed position slightly but he was still asleep, his long legs splayed akimbo on the navy-and-green-plaid bedspread.

Carol went out to the sofa and curled up to wait the two hours before dosing him with the medication.

When Tay awoke early the next morning, he could move freely. His lower back was still sore, and felt tender, as if the wrong move might set him off again, but he was able to sit up on the edge of the bed and take stock of the situation.

He had a vague memory of swallowing pills and water in the night, but confused by a fog of pain and medication, he wasn't sure how much time had passed or what had really happened. He got up and walked gingerly into the hall, hanging on to objects along the way for security. When he got to the living room he saw Carol on the sofa, asleep, the book she had been reading folded open on the floor. She had taken the alarm clock from his nightstand and set it on the cocktail table, obviously using it to time his doses of medication throughout the night.

Tay stood looking down at the sleeping woman, at the long dark lashes, the slender curve of her jaw, the glossy, almost-black hair. How could he feel so much for someone he had known such a short time? Was he just lonely? Had he been too isolated since Alice's death? Some part of him wanted to believe that this pull toward Carol was just circumstantial, but he had never been able to lie to himself. He'd had plenty of opportunities for a relationship since his wife was killed and he had avoided them all. This was new. Carol got under his skin; all she had to do was look at him and he wanted to take her to bed. He had loved Alice, of course, but they had both been kids when they'd met. He was a kid no longer, and he was having trouble resisting the most elemental call a man can experience, no matter how much it might interfere with his future plans.

What was he going to do about her?

He lowered himself into the chair across from Carol and waited for her to waken, in no hurry.

He liked looking at her.

Carol sighed and opened her eyes, her face remaining blank until she had focused on Tay and registered who he was. Then she sat bolt upright and said, "You shouldn't be out of bed!"

"Yes, I should. I'm much better." He moved carefully to her side, sitting on the edge of the sofa. "I can't believe you stayed the night here."

"I couldn't leave you alone."

"I don't deserve such attention."

Carol was silent.

"Aren't you going to say you would have done the same for anybody?"

"I wouldn't have done the same for anybody," she said softly, looking up at him.

His eyes held hers for a long moment and then he said, "I'm going to take a shower and then I'll take you home."

"You can't take a shower! What if you fall?"

"I'm not going to fall. I've been through this several times before, Carol. It's just a muscle spasm and it passes in ten to twelve hours, but before it does, you're paralyzed. Believe me, I'm fine now."

Carol shook her head. "All right, Tay. I'm not going to argue with you. I saw the coffeemaker in the kitchen, I'll go and use it."

"The coffee's in the cabinet just above it," Tay said as she walked away from him.

He went into the bathroom and started the shower, stripping off the clothes he had put on twenty-four hours earlier. He winced as he dropped them into the hamper; he perspired heavily when in pain and now smelled like a cattle pen. He felt a twinge in his back as he stepped under the rushing water, but it subsided as the steaming flood pounded into his muscles, soothing and relaxing them. He soaped and rinsed, then shaved, wiping the fogged mirror with a towel and then wrapping it around his waist. His robe was in the bedroom and as he stepped into the hall to get it, Carol appeared with a mug of coffee in her hand.

They both stopped short.

"I—I thought you were still in the shower," Carol stammered. "I was going to leave this in the bedroom for you."

"Thanks," he said huskily, taking the cup from her hand and setting it on a hall table.

Carol backed up a step. "I guess I'd better...uh..."

Tay leaned forward and put his hand on her arm.

"Please don't touch me," Carol whispered. "All of this has been difficult enough..."

"It's not going to be difficult anymore," Tay replied, bending to slide one arm under her knees and lifting her into his arms.

"Tay, your back!" Carol gasped as he kicked open the bedroom door.

"To hell with my goddamn back," he muttered, and carried her to the bed.

He couldn't think of anything except how much he wanted her. When a trickle of water ran down his arm and she licked it, the touch of her warm tongue on his skin inflamed him. He bent his head and ran his lips along the supple line of her throat as she sank her fingers into the wealth of wet hair at the nape of his neck. He sprawled full-length on the bed with her in his arms, then sat up to unbutton her blouse.

"Do you hear that?" Carol asked faintly, sitting up.

"I don't hear anything," he muttered, unhooking the front closure of her bra.

"It's knocking. There's someone at the door."

He lifted his head. "It's a quarter to seven—a.m."

"I know what time it is, Tay, but there's still someone at the door."

Tay listened for a long moment, then looked down, muttering something he was glad she couldn't hear under his breath.

"Stay here," he said grimly.

He slid off the bed, still clad only in the towel, which had miraculously stayed in place. He shrugged into his robe and pulled the bedroom door closed behind him.

Padding barefoot across the kitchen floor, he yanked open the outer door.

"Hi," Mike said. "You okay?"

"Sure, why not?"

"Well," the workman said, "my cousin Gloria is one of the triage nurses at Avalon General and she called me last night and told me you came into the emergency room on her shift. I've been trying to call here ever since but got no answer."

"Yeah, well, something must be wrong with the phone. I just had a back problem, but it's cleared up now."

"You sure?"

"Positive. I'll be at the site later. Thanks for coming by to check on me, but I'm okay."

Mike shrugged. "All right, Tay. I guess I'll see you at the Lansing house."

Tay watched as Mike jogged down the stairs and got into his truck. Then he went back inside to Carol.

"That was Mike, from my crew," Tay said, sitting next to her on the bed.

"And?"

Tay ran a hand through his now-drying hair. "It turns out that Mike's cousin was the triage nurse on duty at the hospital last night. I didn't even notice her, but she saw me, and she told Mike. He said he's been calling here all night."

"I unplugged the phone. I wanted you to sleep."

He smiled. "I slept."

Carol looked at him, waiting.

"I think I have some explaining to do."

Carol nodded.

"I'd like to pick you up tonight and take you to dinner. Is eight okay?"

Carol smiled. "Eight is fine, if you're sure that you'll be all right."

"I'm sure. I have to go for an X ray this morning. That tyrant at the hospital wouldn't give me a prescription if I didn't promise to come in. They want to look for torn ligaments or something. Can I drop you off at your place on the way?"

"You can drop me off at my place on the way."

He picked up her hand and kissed it, startling her with the tenderness of the gesture.

"Thanks for taking such good care of me," he said.

"You're welcome."

"There's a couple of things I should tell you, Carol."

"What?"

"There's nothing between me and Madeline. Never was."

"Oh."

"And that day you invited me inside for coffee, and for lunch? I showed up alone because I knew your friend Jane wasn't going to be there. I overheard her saying so when she left the previous afternoon."

Carol smiled.

"I guess I'd better get dressed," he said, and grinned at her over his shoulder as he left the room.

* * *

When Jane arrived for their study session, Carol was trying on a dress to wear that evening. She quickly shrugged out of it and tossed it back into the closet.

She didn't want Jane to know about her upcoming date with Tay. It was too private, too personal, to subject to Jane's lighthearted banter.

Carol knew that she was already falling in love with Tay Kirkland.

"I have a news bulletin about your boy," Jane said, poking her head into the bedroom.

Carol looked at her. "What a surprise. Do tell."

"Don't I even get a cup of coffee?"

"It's in the pot in the kitchen, where it always is. What's the news?"

"Ah, we're interested, yes?" Jane said as they went into the other room. She filled a mug and then sat at the kitchen table, sporting a faint, superior smile. "One of the waitresses in Cater's told me quite a bit."

"Jane, if you gave the help in that restaurant the third degree, I will kill you."

"I didn't give anyone the third degree, I just stopped in there last night with Julie Campbell for a sandwich and mentioned that Tay Kirkland was doing the work on your house. This woman Betty was very eager to talk, believe me. Tay's story is a local legend. It turns out that he married Alice Mayfield."

"Who's that?"

"The only child of Chester Mayfield. Mayfield China and Glass?"

Carol was beginning to get the idea. "That's a big company, right?"

"Very big. As in, international. Many bucks."

"And the rich parents weren't happy about their daughter's love life?"

"You said it. It seems the family had a summer home in Avalon and Tay was the lifeguard at the beach there. Alice and Tay fell in love, met on the sly, dodged the threats and defied the daddy—the whole Romeo and Juliet thing. It was quite the talk when it happened. Betty, the waitress, graduated from high school with Tay and she said the two of them were so gorgeous together you didn't know which one to look at first. Once the girl turned eighteen they eloped."

"And the family cut her off," Carol said.

Jane nodded. "The two of them lived here while Tay built his business. They had a child, a girl, and by all reports were very happy."

"Then Alice was killed."

"Right. The grandparents then reared their ugly heads and sued for custody of the kid. And as you've probably guessed, they won."

Carol shook her head. "How?"

"Nobody knows. Tay is like the sphinx about it, but stories have been flying about him ever since it happened. Drugs, alcohol, child abuse..."

"Oh, come on, Jane. You've met the man, can you credit any of that? All he does is work."

"Maybe he was different back then. Maybe he reformed after the wife died. How did the in-laws get the kid, Carol? You know the law. It's awfully hard to take a minor child away from a biological parent if that parent wants to keep it."

Carol was silent. Jane was right.

"So ever since he lost the little girl he's been working like a demon and not saying a word about any of it," Jane continued. "Rumor has it that he got into a fight with some guy who dared to ask him about it a year ago.... Speaking of Tay, where is he?''

"He had an appointment this morning."

"Well, so do we. With *Laidlaw's Bar Review*, if I may change the subject to a less fascinating one. I have all four volumes of that work right here, and Julie says it's the best overview, it really helped her when she took the test. She passed on the first try, I might add."

Carol wasn't listening.

Jane tapped the top book with a nail. "Come on, Carol. Time is short. Forget Blondie for a few hours and get with me on this."

Carol looked back at her friend and nodded. Evening would come, as it always did, and then she would see Tay.

Six

Carol changed clothes three times before she was ready to meet Tay that evening. She hadn't brought a vast wardrobe with her from New York, so the choice was limited, but she finally settled on an ivory silk shirtwaist that would be suitable for almost any situation. She put her hair up in a twist and added small gold hoops to her ears. By comparison with her usual studying wardrobe of shorts and a T-shirt, she was dressed up, and her heeled pumps added to the picture. She felt feminine and capable, but nervous. Very nervous.

Tay was on time. A sleek, dark blue sports car glided to the curb in front of Carol's house at five minutes to eight. She watched in surprise as Tay emerged from it; she had thought he was permanently grafted to his truck. He was dressed in a brown twill jacket, tan slacks and a cream patterned tie. She went to the door to answer it and smiled as her eyes met Tay's.

"Did a fairy godmother change your truck into that glamorous machine?" she asked.

"I use it so rarely I forget that I have it," he replied. "You look beautiful."

"Thank you." Carol took Tay's extended hand and went with him to the car, where he opened the passenger door for her before walking around to get into the driver's seat. Soft music came from the tape deck and the low hum of the motor soothed Carol's jitters as they pulled out of her lane and onto the main drag.

"Where are we going?" Carol asked.

"Just to Avalon. There's a restaurant there called Rosemarie's. Ever heard of it?"

Carol nodded. "My father used to go there often when he was staying at the shore house."

"It has very good Italian food. I made a reservation for eight-thirty."

"Okay."

Tay looked across at her. "I've been pretty mysterious about everything, haven't I? My past. My life. Why I left you hanging that night you saw me at Cater's."

"Yes."

He turned onto the bridge that led over to the mainland. "I never meant to be. You just took me by surprise, that's all."

"Surprise?" Carol said.

"My reaction to you took me by surprise," he clarified.

"Oh," Carol said softly.

"I wasn't prepared for what it would do to my life, my priorities. For so long I've lived for just one thing—to build my business up enough to get my daughter back."

Carol was silent.

"I told you my little girl wasn't with me," he added. "She's with my late wife's parents."

Carol watched the sign indicating the distance to Avalon pass by in a blur as she waited for him to continue.

"They have custody. I have limited visitation rights."

"I'm sorry," Carol said.

"It's a long story, and I won't bore you with the details. Alice's parents were opposed to our marriage, to the point where they tried to have me arrested on various pretexts while we were dating. They accused me of all sorts of things, started rumors, some of which still survive. It was pretty ugly. They thought I was after Alice's money. The family was wealthy and they used all of their power and influence to keep us apart. But we got married anyway, and to show them they were wrong about my motives in pursuing their daughter, I started my own business, working very hard to expand it and make us independent. It worked, I did well, and Alice broke with her parents completely. She was furious with them for trying to get me into trouble and for trying to dictate her life."

"Was the rift ever healed?" Carol asked.

He shook his head. "Alice died without ever speaking to them again. They couldn't seem to get over her defiance of their will in marrying me, even while she was still alive and there was a chance for them to forgive and forget. My business became more successful, but it didn't allay their fears about me, it enraged them. I guess they wanted us to be impoverished so we would have to go crawling back to them and ask them for help. Then they would have the satisfaction of saying to Alice, 'I told you so.'"

"They don't sound like very nice people, Tay," Carol observed quietly.

"They're very powerful people. After a while, powerful people who can buy just about whatever they want forget what it's like to hear the word no."

"But they couldn't force their daughter to give you up," Carol said.

"No, and they never forgave me for that. When they realized that their chance to reconcile with Alice was gone forever, all their bitterness and pain over that situation was channeled into their vendetta against me."

"Vendetta?"

"Within days of Alice's funeral I received papers indicating that they were suing for custody of Alicia."

"On what grounds?"

"On the grounds that I was now a single parent, away working most of the day, with a seasonal and unsteady job, and that I had alienated the affections of their only grandchild."

Carol sighed.

"It was a chance for them to start over again, you see, with Alice's child, and to get back at me at the same time. From their point of view, it was perfect."

Tay was silent a moment, remembering, then said, "I fought it, of course, but I was beaten before I began. They had more lawyers and better lawyers than I did. And, of course, they could show superior financial resources, a more impressive living situation, plans to send Alicia to the best schools—the whole nine yards. I made a good living, but I certainly couldn't compare to them in terms of what I could offer. The judge was an older guy, their age, who obviously looked upon me as some bleached-blond beach stud out of a surfer movie who had stolen the Mayfields' daughter. He made sure he paid me back for that crime."

"Oh, Tay."

His mouth tightened grimly as he turned into the driveway of the restaurant. "I appealed the decision, but it was useless. I spent every cent I had trying to get the decision reversed, and then had to start over when it was clear that I wasn't going to get my daughter back. It has taken me five years to get into a position where a new lawyer might take my case."

"Why so long?"

"I have to show a strong enough track record in my business to indicate that Alicia would not undergo any financial hardship living with me. I have to be able to pay for the private school and the piano lessons and the horseback riding and everything else she has with the Mayfields. I also have to have enough money to interest the kind of lawyer I need, one who can stand up to the stable of gray-haired eminence types Alice's parents will trot out in force to argue their case."

"Your daughter is seven now?"

"Yes," Tay said as they got out of the car and he handed his keys to the valet. He took Carol's elbow and steered her onto the walk that led up to the main door, a path flanked by well-trimmed bushes strung with tiny white lights. The fragrance of the flowering plants surrounded them, and Carol could just hear the sound of pounding surf from the ocean a few blocks away.

"So Alicia would have been two when you lost custody?" Carol asked as they paused under the canvas canopy that bore the restaurant's name in fancy script.

"That's right."

"Does she know who you are when she sees you?" Carol asked him.

Tay pushed open the glass door in front of them. "Oh, sure," he replied bitterly. "She calls me 'Daddy,' sometimes 'Daddy Tay.' I'm sure the Mayfields do everything they can to make her think of her grandfather as her 'real' father."

"She was only two, Tay, what can you expect?" Carol said softly as the maître d' approached them.

Tay interrupted the conversation until they were seated at a quiet table near a window, then leaned across the vase of flowers between them to say, "I know she was only two, Carol, but those people have robbed me of my child! I would have taken care of her—nobody loved her more than I did. When they got custody, Alice's parents hardly knew her! Just because they had more money than I did and the judge was an old fogey who thought I was a kid, she was turned over to the Mayfields. I was powerless. I couldn't do a thing about it. What kind of a system permits something like that?"

"Custody battles are the most painful cases in the law, Tay. Somebody always comes away from them wounded for life."

"And the wounded somebody is usually the one with the least cash in the bank," he said cynically.

Carol said nothing.

"You can't tell me Alice's parents would have gotten Alicia if they were workaday people who collected a salary each week," Tay went on, not looking at Carol. "The social workers, the lawyers, the judges, they were all impressed with the Mayfield bankroll. Of course the almighty Mayfields would be able to do better for the child than her father, who built porches for a living. What a joke. I don't know why I even bothered."

"You bothered because you loved your daughter," Carol said. "You still do."

"Much good it did me."

"It will do Alicia good, because when she gets older she will understand how hard you fought to keep her."

"Not if the Mayfields have anything to say about it," he replied darkly.

The waiter appeared at their table and asked for their wine order. Tay requested a bottle of wine and then sought Carol's gaze with his own, his eyes flashing in the dim restaurant lighting.

"They're trying to cut me out of her life, Carol, I can sense it happening. She talks about their friends and their house and their life, the vacations and the tennis tournaments and the spotted pony. I know they're raising her to think of me as some mistake her mother made when she was very young and didn't know any better. Pretty soon she will be reluctant to see me, then she'll be ashamed of me. The process is inevitable."

"Unless you do something first," Carol interjected.

He nodded. "I'm working on that right now. I had an appointment last week with an attorney I might use, and I plan to interview some others. I'm going to make sure that I don't get outgunned this time." He picked up his menu and handed the second one to Carol. "I'm sorry to bore you with all the grim details, but..."

"I wasn't bored. It's a tragedy. My heart breaks for you, Tay. I can't imagine what it must be like to lose a child that way, especially after just losing your wife."

"I thought I would go insane," he said flatly. "I just worked all the time. I couldn't stand to go home because suddenly no one was there."

The wine came, and Tay left it sitting in its bucket as a waiter took their order. Carol picked items at random; she had never felt less hungry in her life.

"So that's my sad story," Tay said, smiling slightly. "What's yours?"

"Not nearly as sad, I'm relieved to say. Just dull."

He smiled wider. "How could a woman who looks like you have led a dull life?" he asked.

"I've managed it," she said ruefully, and he laughed.

"Come on. No boyfriends?"

"A few. Nobody like..." She had been about to say, *Nobody like you,* but stopped herself in time.

"Like?" Tay asked.

Carol shrugged. "Nobody I'd want to spend the rest of my life with, that's for sure."

"And I've been married to blueprints and supply orders for five years," Tay said softly.

Carol met his eyes and the silence lengthened.

Their waiter arrived with their appetizers and the moment passed.

"What is that?" Carol asked as Tay dug into his.

"Stuffed artichoke," he replied. "Want to try it?"

"No, thanks. I'll stick to my shrimp," Carol replied.

"My wife had champagne tastes," he said, "which she was always trying to duplicate on our beer budget. She liked artichokes, but we were never able to stuff them with some of the items she preferred—caviar, Brie, prawn salad." He paused with his fork in midair. "I was just getting to the point where supplying all of that was a real possibility when she died."

Carol studied his face and then asked in a low tone, "How did it happen?"

"She skidded on a rain-slick road. Nobody's fault. That was almost the worst part of it, there was nobody to blame. Just a stupid, senseless accident. She went out to buy more fabric for some curtains she was making and I never saw her again."

"How awful."

"I used to go over it and over it in my mind, asking myself how it happened. Did she look away for one moment, misjudge the curve, bend down to get something she had dropped? It was maddening, not knowing."

"Do you still feel that way?"

"Sometimes. Mostly in dreams, nightmares. I see the car spinning out of control, hear the crash...." He looked away.

Carol set down her fork.

"I'm sorry," he said, looking back at her. "I'm putting you off your food."

"Not at all. I've had enough."

"You ate one shrimp," he said.

"Two," Carol protested.

"You'll hurt Rosemarie's feelings," Tay said. "Not to mention mine."

Carol speared another shrimp and ate it.

"That's better."

By the time the waiter brought their main course, Tay had opened the wine and poured some for both of them. Carol left hers untouched. She wanted to be clearheaded for the rest of this important evening.

"Is that something else exotic?" Carol asked, gesturing toward Tay's plate.

"I don't consider artichokes exotic," Tay replied.

"What is it you're eating now, Tay?"

"Squid."

"Oh, dear. I knew it. Why don't you just get lasagna like everybody else?"

"Lasagna's too mundane, too pedestrian."

"Aren't you the man who was afraid of my lemon chicken?" Carol asked archly.

"I trust Rosemarie."

"Thanks a lot."

"Well, she's been cooking for me for a long time. Even when I was married, whenever we could afford it we would come here, like for a celebration or something."

"It sounds like you were very happy."

"We were. We came here the night we got the news that Alice was pregnant."

Carol pushed her fork around in her food for a moment and then said, "I think your relationship with Alice would be a tough act to follow."

"For a long time I didn't think it would be possible to find someone else."

Carol looked up at him. "What was she like?"

"Not like you," he said, answering Carol's question right off the bat.

"What do you mean?" Carol asked, her heart sinking.

"She wasn't capable, independent. She had been raised as an only child in an atmosphere of privilege, she'd had everything done for her. It was a terrible adjustment for her to find that support system gone and to have to do everything for herself."

"But she did it for you," Carol said.

"Well, we were kids. Anything seemed possible then." He nodded toward her plate. "Don't you like that?"

"It's very good. I guess I'm not very hungry after all."

Tay shook his head. "You don't eat enough to keep a bird alive. Do you want me to ask the waiter to take that away and bring you something else?"

"No, I'm fine. Just some coffee, thanks."

Tay signaled for the waiter. "You and that buddy of yours live on coffee. Haven't you ever heard of caffeine nerves?"

"Nobody gets through law school without coffee. Or something worse."

Tay gave their order and then said to Carol, "Is it really that bad?"

"It's not easy. Plenty of stress, especially in the first year. The professors are trying to see if you can take the pressure of a courtroom, so they supply quite a bit of their own. If you make it through that, it gets easier, but a lot of people don't. And the workload remains staggering, no matter what stage of study you happen to be in, until the end."

"Why did you stick with it?"

"Orneriness?" she suggested, and he laughed.

"Seriously, my father didn't think I would be able to stay the course, and I was determined to prove that I could."

"Why didn't he think you could do it?"

"It was more like he didn't want me to do it. He preferred women to look up to him, not compete with him. But he accepted my career in the end and came to my graduation."

"Did your mother look up to him?"

"She made him think she did. She was very smart, but she used her intelligence to flatter his ego and get him to do what she wanted. I was determined to be more upfront about my abilities."

"Two different generations," Tay said quietly.

"Yes, I guess so."

Their coffee came and they sipped companionably for a while, then Carol asked, "When are you going to refile for custody of your daughter?"

"As soon as I settle on a lawyer."

"Good luck."

"I'll need it." Tay changed the subject to the work he was doing on the house, and by the time they left the restaurant he had fallen silent, seemingly preoccupied during the drive back to Strathmere.

Carol was about to ask Tay what she had done to cause his change in mood when he said, "I'd like to come in for a moment when we get to your place. Is that all right?"

"Of course."

He pulled up in front of her house and then opened the door for Carol to emerge from his car. She tried to read his face as they walked up to her door, but his expression was carefully impassive. He stood back as she unlocked the front door, then he followed her inside.

"Would you care for anything?" Carol asked as he pulled his tie loose from its knot.

He shook his head, waiting for her to sit. She did so, and then he followed suit, taking the spot opposite her on the rattan sofa. Carol watched as he opened his mouth, then closed it again, finally saying, "This is hard."

"What is? Please tell me, Tay, you're scaring me."

"I can't see you any more after tonight," he said quietly.

Carol stared at him in amazement, unable to reply.

"I've explained the situation with my daughter, but there was one thing I didn't tell you."

Carol swallowed, her eyes on his face.

"The lawyer I saw told me I can't have an intimate relationship with anyone. It's the first thing the Mayfields will use if I bring them back into court. They'll say that I'm sleeping around. That I'm promiscuous and risking my health. That it's an indication of my irresponsibility. That I would provide an immoral atmosphere for the child. You know the arguments, you've probably used them in the past yourself when preparing cases."

"But if we just see each other and don't..."

"That's impossible, Carol. You know it and I know it. No matter how hard we tried sooner or later we would—" He stopped and shrugged.

"How long have you known this?" Carol whispered.

"All along. I'd had advice earlier. The lawyer just confirmed what I already knew. That's why I tried to stay away from you, remember?"

"I remember that you sought me out and came to this house," Carol said bitingly.

"That was a mistake. I just couldn't stay away."

"So let me understand this," Carol said. "You took me on this date to tell me there would be no more dates?"

Tay was silent.

"I asked you a question."

"Yes," he said.

"How kind of you. I must say that this is a very elaborate and gracious kiss-off, but no doubt you felt you owed it to me after taking certain, uh, liberties, shall we say?"

"You were very eager to participate, as I recall," Tay said tightly.

"How dare you say that to me!" Carol said, her eyes filling with tears against her will as her anger rose. "You knew all along it could lead to nothing. You knew all along that any relationship with me would jeopardize your case for your daughter, and yet you pursued me!"

"I wanted you. I want you now."

"I don't care what you want! What are you, five years old? You see a pretty toy and you must have it?" Carol stood abruptly and wiped her eyes furtively with the back of her hand. Striving for a calmer tone, she said, "I can understand fully that getting your daughter back is the most important thing in your life. It would be for me, too. And I also know you're right in assuming that the

Mayfields will use any relationship you're having against you. If I were their lawyer I would give them the very same advice. What I can't understand is how you could forget about all of that for one moment and come after me so ardently when you knew that it had to end like this!''

"I wasn't thinking—" he said helplessly.

"Then start thinking now! Don't you realize the cruelty of what you've done? You rope me in, you make me care for you, you present me with a generous sample of what I will be missing, and then you cut me off like a— like a football player whose prospective girlfriend failed to make the cheerleading squad!"

"Carol, don't—" Tay said, rising abruptly and making a move toward her.

Carol held up her hand. "You led me on. I didn't know your situation, but you did, the whole time. You should have stayed away from me."

"If our positions were reversed, could you have stayed away from me?" he asked rhetorically.

Carol faced him, fresh tears welling up in her eyes.

"Then do it now," she whispered. "What you weren't able to do before, do now. Stay away from me."

"Carol, I don't want it to end this way—"

"Of course not. You want me to make you feel better about what you've done, but I'm not going to cooperate. I don't want to see you outside of the work you're doing on the house. God knows, I hope that's over very soon. Don't speak to me, don't call me, don't contact me at all for anything. If you have a message to convey, you can do it through John Spencer. Now go."

Tay didn't move.

"You heard me," Carol said.

Tay turned slowly, then looked back at her over his shoulder and opened his mouth.

"Go!" Carol repeated.

He walked across the living room and let himself out the door quietly.

Carol stared after him for a moment and then put her face in her hands.

Tay looked at the bedside clock and then back at the ceiling. It was 3:00 a.m., he hadn't slept at all, and he had to be up at seven. But he was wide awake, jacked on adrenaline, the aftermath of the scene with Carol.

Tay rubbed his eyes wearily. He kept replaying the evening's end in his mind, hoping that he would come off better each time. But he never did. Everything that Carol had said was the simple truth, and he knew it.

He rolled over and pressed his face into the pillow, trying to blot out the image of her stricken expression. How could he have been such an idiot? He had let it go too far, like a kid saying "Just one more piece of candy...just one more TV show until bedtime...just one more day." And now she was justifiably furious. But he couldn't go into court and make himself vulnerable to the accusations the Mayfields would surely bring against him. They would have him under surveillance the minute they received the legal papers, and any private investigator would uncover a relationship with Carol in a day or two. His only chance was to make sure that there was nothing to find.

Tay punched the pillow and kicked off his sheet. It wasn't fair. No man should be forced to make such a choice. But he wasn't going to give up on getting Alicia back after he had been working on it for five years. A little more time and the courts would say that she should stay where she had been placed, that any disruption would be bad for her development. He had to act now.

He rolled over again and stared once more at the ceiling.

Seven

A merciful fate decided that it should rain for the next several days, so Tay's crew did not show up at Carol's house. Jane decided not to brave the weather and since several of the other homes on the street were empty Carol was left alone to study and to collect her thoughts.

Those thoughts were not happy. She tried to put Tay out of her mind, but he surfaced at the most inopportune moments: when she attempted to focus on a graph or chart, when she tried to read some of her notes and the handwriting blurred on the page, when she listened to audio tapes and the lecturer's voice was replaced by Tay's. She knew she shouldn't be wasting a moment's time on him, but he was not so easily forgotten. Even her dreams were invaded; her sleep was disrupted by disturbing images that dissolved like mist when she awoke.

The idea of taking the bar exam loomed like the prospect of doom.

On the fourth day of continuous rain the phone rang while Carol was taking a bath, the textbook on Federal Income Taxation propped on the rim of the tub. Muttering to herself as the wind rattled the windows and the rain drummed on the roof, she picked up a towel and wrapped it around her body. She tiptoed across the bathroom tiles, leaving wet footprints in her wake, and went into the bedroom, picking up the receiver with a damp hand.

"Hello?"

"Carol, it's Jane. Have you had the television or the radio on today?"

"No, I've been studying."

"That's what I thought. There have been storm warnings broadcast all morning. Haven't you noticed that the wind is picking up?"

"Yeah, I guess it's pretty windy," Carol replied, looking through the window at the trees whipping past the glass.

"Pretty windy! Since last night the gale has increased to hurricane force and they're expecting the worst storm in several years."

"So? I should find a partner and head for the ark?"

"So you'd better get out of there! You're on a peninsula that has gone under several times in the past. In the big storm of the 1920s four blocks were lost in the ocean. Haven't you ever noticed that the street numbers begin at the stoplight on the corner of Fifth, not First?"

"Where am I going to go?"

"Come and stay with me."

"And drive through all this rain?"

"It's better than swimming through it. I'm not kidding, Carol, you'd better put on the TV and track the evacuation information. Look out the window. Do you see cars in any of the other driveways on the street?"

Carol peered through the curtain. "Not really."

"They're probably all gone already. They don't know you, Carol. You're not a regular resident, they think of you as summer people. They would just leave and assume you heard the warnings broadcast in the media."

"All right, all right," Carol said. "I'll pack a bag and drive over to your place."

"Do it now, before the storm gets any worse," Jane said, and hung up the phone with a bang.

Carol went back to the bathroom, sluiced off the remaining bubble bath in the shower, and then got dressed. She was stuffing underwear into a backpack and folding her raincoat over her arm when she heard pounding on her front door.

She went into the living room and looked out the window. A utility truck with flashing lights was parked at the foot of her driveway. Through the pelting rain she could see several men in yellow slickers setting up barricades at the end of her street. Sighing deeply, she pulled open her door.

Tay was standing on her front steps, wearing a navy hooded sweatshirt soaked to black, his hair plastered to his forehead, water dripping off the end of his nose.

As soon as Carol saw who was out there she started to shut the door.

Tay stuck his foot in the jamb.

"Get lost," Carol said firmly, still trying to close the door on his leg.

"Carol, you have to get out of here, they're cutting off access to the street."

"So what the hell do you care? You work for public service now?"

"I came here because I thought you would be stubborn enough to stay here when everyone else had left, and it looks like I was right,'' he answered, shoving his way inside.

"For your information I wasn't being stubborn, I just didn't have the TV or the radio on, so I didn't know about the storm warnings.''

"That's just like you—isn't it?—to be so much in your own world that not even an approaching hurricane gets through the fog. Did you even notice that it was raining?''

"Of course I noticed that it was raining. It's been raining for four days. I was very grateful that the bad weather kept you away from here. That reminds me, get out of my house,'' Carol said, folding her arms.

"I'm not leaving unless it's with you.''

"If you think you're taking me anywhere, you've lost your mind,'' Carol replied.

"We'll see about that,'' he said, his expression grim.

"I was going to leave anyway.''

"Do you mind if I don't take your word for that?''

"Why, are you assuming that I'm as dishonest as you are?'' Carol snapped back at him.

Tay wiped his wet face with the back of his hand and said patiently, as if he hadn't heard her, "Are you going to come with me willingly or am I going to carry you?''

Carol stared at him. "You wouldn't dare.''

He stared right back at her. "Try me.''

Carol was silent.

"Think about it. Do you want all those hard-working municipal employees out there to see you dragged, kicking and screaming like a whore in a bordello roundup, out the door and then into my truck? Or will you proceed in a ladylike fashion down the steps under your own steam?''

"Where?" Carol asked shortly, accepting the inevitable.

"My place."

"You really are insane," she said dismissively, turning away from him. "I'm going to Jane's."

"No, you're not. If you haven't been listening to the bulletins you don't know that the bridge is closed and all access to the mainland is cut off as of a few minutes ago. If you don't want to stay with me your choice is the XCel Motel, and I think it should be pretty booked by now."

Carol sighed in defeat. "Why is the bridge closed?"

"The south seawall collapsed, everyone on this side of the strip is being moved. My place is on a slight elevation in the center, it should be safe there."

Carol felt trapped and frustrated, but she picked up her bag and zipped it closed.

"I'm leaving the second it's okay to go," she said.

"Fine."

"This doesn't change anything between us."

"I understand that. Can we end this debate and leave? The water is rising as we speak."

Carol said nothing in reply, but shut off the living room lamp and shrugged into her raincoat, then walked to the door. Tay followed, and then stepped aside as she locked the door behind them. She wasn't sure why she was bothering to lock it, the house would probably be afloat by nightfall. At least it was insured, but she couldn't help thinking about all of Tay's hard work gone to waste. She almost felt sorry for him.

Almost.

When they turned into the wind the rain hit them like a wave, drenching Carol in seconds. She pulled her hood up over her head and dashed for Tay's truck, with him right behind her. They vaulted into the cab and Tay started the motor, which coughed and sputtered a few times before roaring into life.

"Distributor is wet," he said shortly, pulling out into the street.

They had only gone a few feet, gushing water from the tires on either side, before one of the workers at the end of the lane flagged them down.

"Got everything you need?" he shouted at Tay when he rolled down his window. "We're closing this road off right now. It's going to flood any minute and you won't be able to get back in here until the storm is over."

Tay nodded.

"Which way you going?" he asked Tay, jerking his head toward the distance.

"Notch Road, back over to my place," Tay replied.

The man shook his head. "Notch Road's washed out. You'll have to go around Domingo Avenue and then across Norton."

"Okay," Tay replied, raising his voice over the wind. His yellow hazard lights cast an eerie glow through the gloom as the motor of the truck idled under them.

"And stay put once you get there, this is no day to be out driving," the worker shouted.

Tay nodded again and gunned the motor, leaning forward to peer through the streaming windshield. There was no sound in the cab except their breathing and the clicking of the wipers as Tay negotiated past fallen limbs and floating debris, the truck lurching as they hit ruts created by the flooding. Carol realized that he had rescued her from a serious situation when she saw the number of stalled and abandoned vehicles incapacitated by the weather, and the dangling phone and utility wires ripped loose by the wind. She was lucky that she still had power at her house, but she doubted it would be on much longer.

They stopped at a light and the truck stalled. Carol looked anxiously at Tay's face as he tried to start it again and the motor turned over, then failed.

"Don't worry," he said reassuringly when he glanced at her and saw her expression. "If the truck gives out we can make it on foot from here."

Carol nodded. She had an idea of where they were and he was right.

The motor finally caught and held, and they were just gliding slowly across a flooded intersection when Carol saw a young woman stuck with a compact car. Through the fogged window on her side Carol could make out a toddler in the back and an infant strapped into a car seat in the front. She looked over at Tay and saw that he was already turning the wheel.

"I'm going to stop," he said to Carol, carefully edging the truck in behind the compact. Carol did not miss the relief on the young woman's face when she looked up and saw that they were coming to help her.

Tay left the truck motor running and then jumped down from the cab. Carol was getting out on her side, almost blinded by the driving rain, when he appeared in front of her and handed her a warm bundle.

"Hold her," he said, and ran off again. Carol looked down into the cherubic face of a baby girl, who beamed up at her new friend, displaying two perfectly matched lower teeth in a gummy smile. Carol clutched the baby as Tay ran back to the truck with its mother and the toddler. The boy stared at Carol as his mother squeezed in next to her and then took him on her lap.

"Wet," he announced, his knit hat drooping over one eye, and Carol thought, Yes, indeed.

"Thank you so much," the young woman gasped. "My car is dead and I had no idea how I was going to get these two home. The emergency vehicles kept passing me by—I guess there are people in worse trouble—but Tommy tends to wander and I wasn't sure I could walk with him and carry Sarah...."

"Where do you live?" Tay asked, interrupting her nervous monologue.

"Just a few blocks away, but in this weather..."

"Show me," Tay said tersely.

The little boy turned to Carol confidentially and said, "Crying outside."

Carol chuckled and his mother rolled her eyes as she pointed in the direction of her home.

They crawled to their destination, taking about fifteen minutes to negotiate the short distance. Once they pulled into the driveway, Tay hustled both children and their mother into the house in short order. Carol watched as the young woman waved and blew kisses from her doorway, mouthing, "God bless you," as Tay jumped back into the cab.

"You have a fan for life," Carol said to him as he, thoroughly soaked and dripping more water on the floor, pulled the truck out into the street again.

"But not in here, right?" he replied, casting her a sidelong glance.

Carol let that pass, gripping the seat as they banged into a pothole and water seeped under the truck doors.

"That was a big one," Tay said grimly, his knuckles white on the steering wheel.

"Not much further, right?" Carol asked, really getting alarmed now. The sky was an ugly color, gray-black with saffron streaks, the rain unrelenting. She peered around anxiously; they were almost alone on the road.

"Getting close," he replied.

When Tay's garage came into view Carol said a silent prayer of thanks. Tay pulled the truck right to the foot of the steps leading to his apartment and then got out to help Carol from the cab. She hopped down to the wet macadam and then let go of his arm the instant she was sure of her footing.

"Come on," Tay said, squinting at the sky. He sprinted up the stairs and she followed, stepping inside when Tay unlocked the door. Tay pulled the door closed smartly and then held out his hand for Carol's coat.

She took it off and handed it to him, pushing her wet hair back from her face with her free hand. Tay hung her coat on the back of his door. He picked up her bag and said, "You can change in my bedroom if you like."

"Fine." Carol took the bag and went into the bedroom, stripping out of her wet clothes and changing into the jeans and T-shirt she had brought with her. When she went back into the kitchen, Tay had changed into dry clothes also and was pouring whiskey into two glasses.

"I don't want that," Carol said.

"Oh, stop being such a priss. I'm not trying to get you drunk," Tay replied irritably. "Your teeth are chattering."

"Then I'll have a cup of tea," Carol said, moving toward the stove.

He stared at her. "Just what is it that I find so appealing about you?" he asked, sounding puzzled, as if talking to himself. "You're a judgmental killjoy."

"Maybe you've killed the joy in me, Taylor, did you ever think of that?" Carol shot back at him.

He bolted his whiskey and slammed the glass down on the kitchen table. "Why did I even bother stopping over there to pick you up?'' he demanded. ''I should have tossed you a life preserver and kept on driving!''

''Maybe I wish you had!'' Carol retorted, wishing no such thing but feeling the familiar exasperation overtaking her. She still wanted him so much, she had to be constantly on her guard, and now she was in this impossible situation, trapped in the same house with him during a raging storm.

He stomped out of the kitchen and yanked the bedroom door closed. Carol listened to the sound of the rain drumming on the roof and then went into the living room, collapsing on the sofa. She had been there only a few minutes when she heard the phone ringing and then the murmur of Tay's voice in conversation. She looked up when he appeared in the doorway, zipping up a quilted windbreaker.

''I have to go out again,'' he said neutrally.

''What? You just got here!''

''I have earth-moving equipment in the garage and it's needed to clear some of the roads blocked by fallen trees.''

''So let them take it. Why do you have to operate it?''

''Because I know how,'' he replied shortly, and headed for the door.

''Let some of your men do it,'' Carol said.

He ignored her, pulling work gloves out of the pockets of the jacket.

''When will you be back?'' Carol asked anxiously, rising from her seat.

He turned to look at her. ''You almost sound worried about me,'' he said sarcastically, and left, shutting the door a little harder than was necessary.

Carol was left staring at the closed door.

* * *

The rain stopped about ten o'clock that evening, but Carol didn't start to get worried until Tay hadn't returned by midnight. She had left a message for Jane and then spent the time while Tay was gone reading a review text she had brought with her. This proved so stimulating that she fell asleep halfway through it and when she awoke she was still alone.

Carol paced the floor, alternately glancing at the clock and at the television, listening for bulletins on the aftermath of the storm. She was watching a report on flooding along the Jersey shore when she finally heard the door open behind her.

She ran into the kitchen and saw Tay, drenched again, this time also smeared with mud, unlacing his work boots. He looked up and saw her.

"Don't ask," he said.

She didn't.

He unzipped the jacket, which appeared to have grass stains all over it, and then pulled it and the hooded sweatshirt under it over his head. Carol looked away.

Tay padded barefoot to the refrigerator, opened it, and stuck his head inside. When he emerged he was holding a rock-hard, discolored slab of cheese that Carol had examined and rejected earlier in the evening. When he bit into it, she winced.

"I take it there were no snack breaks," Carol said dryly.

He shrugged.

"Would you like an omelet?" she asked.

He looked at her hopefully, then his expression changed. "Flavored with arsenic?" he asked.

"I'll declare a limited truce for the sake of your Good Samaritan tendencies," Carol said, stepping around him to remove a carton of eggs and a stick of butter from the refrigerator. He sat gingerly at the table as she moved to the stove.

"Is your back bothering you again?" she asked sharply.

He smiled slightly. "Carol, my mother in Florida is filling the bill nicely. I don't need two nagging mommies."

"I wasn't nagging, just inquiring."

"I thought you wanted me dead and buried, and here you are feeding me and requesting medical reports."

"You look too tired to be treated as you deserve," Carol replied, cracking eggs.

"You never lack for an answer, do you?" he said.

"Not where you're concerned."

"Well, you'll make a good lawyer."

Carol took the cheese from him and shaved some of it into the eggs, then opened the breadbox to find several hunks of stale bread still wrapped in plastic. She selected two slices and cut the mold off the edges, then popped them into the toaster.

"When was the last time you went grocery shopping?" she said to him, turning the eggs with a spatula.

"Vernal equinox?" he suggested, watching as she turned off the heat and then shifted the omelet to a plate. "When the moon was in the seventh house and Jupiter aligned with Mars?"

"Very funny," Carol said. "Your cheese is about the same age as your bread, roughly Cro-Magnon." She put the plate in front of him and removed the toast from the toaster.

"I bought them the same day. Along with a steak, which could be used as a cricket bat, now residing in my freezer." He dug into the eggs and made appreciative noises, nodding as she added the buttered toast to his plate.

"Didn't your wife ever teach you to cook anything?" Carol asked him.

He shook his head. "You might say her experiments drove both of us into restaurants. She never gave up, though. She was determined. And she did get to be quite good, after a while." He chewed enthusiastically, and Carol felt a pang when she realized how hungry he'd been while working so hard. He looked dead tired, with dark shadows under his eyes and brown beard stubble covering his cheeks and chin. Carol gave him a glass of water as he finished the food, and he drained it.

"You'd better get to bed," she said. "You seem like you're out on your feet."

He got up and went into the bedroom, emerging a few seconds later with a pillow and a blanket.

"What are you doing?" Carol asked.

"I'm going to sleep on the sofa," he replied.

"Oh, no, you're not," Carol said, putting his plate in the sink. "You need a good night's sleep, and—"

"Please don't argue with me," he said wearily. "I'm too done-in to hold up my end. Just do what I say for once and take the bed, okay?"

"Okay," Carol murmured meekly, chastened by the finality of his tone. He was in no mood for a debate.

"Good night," he said gruffly, and disappeared into the living room.

Carol trailed dispiritedly into the bedroom and shut the door. She had neglected to bring any sleepwear, so she stripped off her jeans, took off her bra, and climbed into the bed in her T-shirt and panties.

She could not sleep. The atmosphere seemed strangely quiet after the drumming on the roof that had provided constant background noise for the previous several days. The lowering wind's almost inaudible murmuring added to the stillness. But while the storm outside might be over, the storm in Carol's heart was increasing.

How could she sleep when thoughts of the bed's previous occupant filled her mind? His head had rested on this pillow, his body on this sheet. She pressed her nose to the blanket and fancied she smelled his unique, masculine scent. She tossed and sighed until she threw off the thin summer coverlet and went to the window, opening it to look out on a washed-clean world, the fragrance of a summer night rising to greet her.

The neon lights above the doors on Tay's garage showed her branches still dappled with drops, piles of fallen leaves slashed from the trees by the wind, puddles of water not yet dried on the paved driveway. She inhaled deeply of the fresh air and then glanced at the clock—2:00 a.m. She had been tossing for more than an hour.

She decided to go out to the kitchen to get something to drink; she had seen a can of juice in one of the cupboards. She recalled that it was covered with a layer of dust, like most of Tay's other supplies, but if hermetically sealed, it should still be okay. She tiptoed to the door and opened it a crack, careful not to disturb Tay sleeping in the other room.

Carol stopped short as she entered the kitchen, her mouth open in surprise.

Tay was sitting at the kitchen table, wearing the jeans he'd had on earlier, minus the leather belt. A glass with an inch of brown liquid in it sat on the table in front of him and he was smoking a cigarette.

"I assumed you were sleeping," Carol said stupidly.

"Guess again."

"I thought you were exhausted."

"Maybe so, but I can't sleep."

"Why not?"

"Oh, I don't know, perhaps the idea of you curled up in the next room wearing that extremely fetching outfit has something to do with it."

Carol glanced down at herself in embarrassment. The T-shirt was skimpy at best and the panties left little to the imagination. When she looked up again, it was to meet his appraising gaze.

"You didn't know what I was wearing," she said defensively, tugging on the shirt hem.

"I was fairly sure that it was less than what you were wearing before," he replied dryly, inhaling deeply until the tip of the cigarette glowed.

"I didn't know you smoked."

"I used to, but Alice persuaded me to give it up years ago." He exhaled a luxuriant stream of grayish smoke. "I seem to be doing it again."

"Are you under stress?"

He gave a short bark of a laugh.

"Look, Tay," Carol said, "I'm sorry if my presence here is making you uncomfortable, but this visit wasn't my doing, after all. I'll go home as soon as I can—"

He waved her words away with the hand that held the cigarette. "It's not your fault. If you were here or at home or on Venus, I would still be thinking about making love to you."

"Tay, we decided—"

"I know what we decided, damn it, and I know it was my idea. You don't have to tell me, Carol, I remember. I just didn't understand how tough it was going to be. When it was raining and I didn't see you for three days, I almost went crazy with missing you. And then when I

thought you were going to be stranded by the storm..."
He gestured helplessly, his shoulders slumping.

Carol felt her throat tighten. She knew she should be
angry with him for what he had put her through, but he
was obviously so unhappy about their dilemma that her
heart went out to him. She walked over to him and put
her fingers on his bare shoulder. He turned his head and
kissed her hand.

"Please," he whispered hoarsely. "Just this once."

"Tay, we should make a clean break, there's no future
in it," she said painfully, as if by rote, wanting him as
much as he did her.

"I need you," he said, turning toward her, dropping
the cigarette into the glass and wrapping his arms around
her waist. Carol closed her eyes and cradled his head
against her breast. What did it matter if tomorrow the
coming custody battle loomed large in his mind again and
he ran from her once more? She would have the memory
of this night to carry with her forever.

Carol buried her face in his hair, closing her eyes as his
hands slipped under shirt and caressed her naked back.
With one movement he shoved the shirt above her waist
and took her nipple into his mouth. Carol gasped and
dug her nails into his shoulders as his beard raked her
skin.

"I've thought about making love to you for so long,"
he muttered. "From the first day I saw you." He moved
his mouth to her other breast, leaving a trail of wetness
across her skin. Never losing contact, he bent suddenly
and slipped an arm under her knees, pulling her onto his
lap.

He was fully aroused and Carol felt him hard against
her as he lifted his head and kissed her mouth. She tasted
the bitterness of tobacco on his lips, the tang of whiskey,

and then she was lost, her lips opening under his as he rose with her in his arms and carried her into the next room. He set her on the edge of the bed and she pulled him down with her.

He kissed her again, deeply, searchingly, and then pulled her shirt over her head, dropping it on the floor. Carol wound her arms around his neck as he kissed her shoulders, her throat, and finally her breasts again, sucking and nipping until Carol was moaning steadily. She lay under him, her hands roaming over his arms and back, marveling at the softness of his skin and the hardness of the muscles flexing beneath it. When he lowered his head and tongued her navel, she whimpered and lifted her hips toward him. He gripped the top of her briefs and ripped them from her body. Carol bit her lip as his mouth trailed over her belly, her hips. When she felt his touch where she most desired it, she gasped out loud and sank her fingers into his hair.

Time slowed, then stopped, as Carol rode a wave of inexpressible pleasure. When he lifted his head she was already tugging wildly at the button on his jeans. He left her for a moment and quickly unzipped his pants, kicking them out of his way. When he returned to her, she wrapped her legs around his hips and took him in her hand.

Tay's breath hissed from between his teeth as his eyes closed. He lowered his face to her shoulder, his skin fiery, his back slick with perspiration.

"Do you like that?" she whispered.

He made an unintelligible sound as she caressed him, his body as taut as a bow.

"Do you want me now?" she said, and he groaned.

"I can't wait any longer, either," Carol said as his seeking hand touched her and found her ready. She dug her heels into him as he lifted her and entered her deeply. She gripped his shoulders and moved with him as they found their own path to fulfillment.

Carol thought Tay was asleep, his head against her shoulder, but when she looked down at him his eyes were open.

"And I thought you were tired," she said, and he smiled.

"What did you do all the time you were gone?" she asked him as he rolled over and settled next to her.

"We were unblocking roads, moving tree stumps and fallen limbs so people could get out."

"Sounds like fun."

He shrugged. "I've worked storms before. It wouldn't have been too bad except it was raining so hard that we could barely see what we were doing."

"Was it the worst storm since you've lived here?" Carol asked him.

"Oh, no, I've seen the whole place flooded out, but this was the kind of driving rain that causes bad accidents." He ran his hand along her hip and said, "This is an historic occasion. First time I've ever made love to a lawyer."

Carol laughed. "Did it feel any different?"

"I don't know how to answer that question. All the other lawyers I know are men."

"Does it bother you?" she asked.

"What?"

"My profession."

"Honey, I was a goner from the moment I saw you. I could have found out afterward that you were an undertaker and it wouldn't have made a difference."

"It's funny how that happens," Carol said softly. "You can go through your whole life and with everybody you meet, it's sort of... pleasant. Not awful, just no fireworks. And then you see that one person and it's..."

"The Fourth of July."

"Right."

He sat up and traced her lips with his forefinger, his expression serious.

"Carol, I..."

She placed her own finger against his mouth. "Shh, don't talk about it. I understand. It was my decision to stay with you. Let's not waste this time with conversation."

She kissed him and he responded, rolling her under him, and the storm began again.

When Carol awoke for the second time the sun was shining through the curtains in Tay's bedroom and she was alone. She sat up against the pillows, enjoying the sight she hadn't seen for several days, thinking of lines from the Bible she remembered from her childhood: For truly the light is sweet, and what a pleasant thing it is for the eyes to see the sun.

It had to be a good omen.

As if to confirm this, Tay came through the door, freshly showered and shaven, wearing a crisp shirt and tan jeans. He handed her a cup of coffee.

"I've been up for several hours, thinking about everything," he said. "And I know what we have to do."

"What's that?" Carol asked.

"Get married."

Eight

Carol stared at him, unable to reply.

"Well?" he said. "Don't you see?"

Carol shook her head.

"The Mayfields won't be able to object to you if we're married. They won't be able to portray you as my floozy or my girlfriend, or our relationship as anything but legitimate. Our marriage would remove that ammunition from their arsenal permanently."

Carol looked away from him.

"What's the matter?" Tay asked. "You're the lawyer. Tell me, isn't that right?"

"Tay, I don't want to marry you in order to thwart the Mayfields," Carol said flatly.

He looked stricken. "You don't want to marry me?" he asked.

"Of course I do. I just want your reason for the wedding to be me, not your daughter."

He sat next to her on the bed and took her hands in his. "I'm sorry if my proposal was less than romantic, I know I put it badly."

"Anyway, I can't get married now."

"Why not?"

"For one thing, I'm due to take the bar exam in a couple of weeks."

"The two events are mutually exclusive?"

"I have to concentrate on the bar, that's enough to deal with until it's over. And for another thing, I'm moving back to New York once you finish the renovations on the house."

"Move in with me instead."

"Tay, I can't, I have to go back to work at Appleton and Smyth at the end of the summer. They're counting on me."

"All right, let's get engaged, then. As long as the commitment between us is there the courts will view the situation positively, and then we can get married as soon as you straighten out your future plans."

Carol looked at him dubiously. He was saying what she had so wanted to hear, but she hadn't envisioned quite this pragmatic scenario.

And he hadn't said that he loved her. He wanted her, he needed her to reclaim his child, but was that enough?

Sensing her mood, he went down on one knee next to the bed and held her hand to his lips.

"Carol, listen to me," he said quietly, his eyes fixed on hers. "I'm so tired of being alone. I'm asking you to marry me and be with me forever. Will you?"

Carol touched his cheek, her eyes filling with tears. "I'll marry you." She leaned forward and wrapped her arms around his neck, pulling him onto the bed.

"When?" he said, nuzzling her neck.

"In a few months, when things are settled. You'll file for custody, I'll go back to New York, and then we'll see."

"I want to do it now," he said thickly, pulling the sheet from her body and running his hand up her thigh.

"Soon," Carol whispered, and then the talking stopped.

Carol felt as if the next couple of months were a whirlwind. The house on Schoolhouse Lane, which only sustained minor damage during the storm, had been put on the market as soon as Tay finished the renovations and repairs. Carol moved back to her apartment in Greenwich Village and resumed her job at Appleton and Smyth in September, just after taking the bar exam. She had no idea how she had done, and had decided not to worry about it until she got the results. She was far too happy.

Tay spent every weekend with her, and Carol helped to prepare his custody case and interview prospective lawyers to handle it. After going with him to several meetings she finally decided that the best candidate was right under her nose.

Harold Smyth, the senior partner of her firm and her boss for the past two years, agreed to take Tay's case after he reviewed the previous custody ruling—and after Carol had assured him that Tay could pay his fees.

Carol was thrilled; not only was Smyth experienced with custody battles, but he had a high-profile name to compare with the Trenton branch of the Brahmin firm the Mayfields employed. Appleton and Smyth might not be old Boston, but they were well known, qualified to practice in New Jersey, and certain to impress a hearing judge. And best of all, Tay's petition for a change of venue was granted on the grounds that the judge in the previous hearing had been a friend of the Mayfields' lawyer. The case was now set for Ocean rather than Atlantic County, and Tay was hopefully looking forward to the hearing.

Carol was working in her cubbyhole at Appleton and Smyth one afternoon in late September when Smyth's secretary poked her head into the small office and told Carol that she had a visitor, a Mr. Bartholomew Reed.

Puzzled, Carol rose and followed the woman to the conference room down the hall. The name of her visitor sounded familiar but she couldn't place it. She stared in surprise at the exquisitely tailored, handsome older man with iron-gray hair and green eyes who rose from the leather chair to greet her.

"Miss Lansing, how do you do?" he said, extending his hand as the secretary closed the door behind them, leaving them alone. "I'm Bartholomew Reed. I am representing Chester and Regina Mayfield in the custody matter regarding their granddaughter. I would like to speak with you about the case."

Carol shook his hand. "I think you have been misinformed, Mr. Reed," Carol replied, kicking herself mentally for not recognizing his name immediately from the court papers. "Mr. Harold Smyth is representing the plaintiff in that case, you should speak to him. I've not yet been admitted to the bar."

Reed smiled. "Come now, Miss Lansing, let's be frank. Your modesty is becoming but a little disingenuous, don't you think? Harold Smyth would not have taken the Kirkland case except for your intervention."

"You're very well informed, Mr. Reed."

"It's a necessity of our profession. I understand that you have a personal relationship with Taylor Kirkland."

"We're engaged, Mr. Reed, that's common knowledge, but I am not going to discuss that with you."

"The hearing judge might find your affianced status interesting," Reed said thoughtfully.

"I am not the attorney of record, Mr. Reed, as I have already pointed out to you. I am assisting on the case as an intern, and if you want to make something of that in court, I invite you to try. Now, if there's nothing else, I'm very busy." Carol tried to edge past him toward the door.

Reed's glacial eyes narrowed. "I wonder if you've considered, Miss Lansing, that Taylor Kirkland's interest in you might not be as forthright as it seems."

"I beg your pardon?" Carol replied, her tone as frosty as Reed's stare.

"Your presence in his life has rendered him a great service in the preparation of his case, not to mention allowing him to present to the judge the prospect of a stable family unit with two parents as well as a double income."

"This interview is over, Mr. Reed," Carol said, turning her back on him.

He reached around her to put a detaining hand on her arm. "Taylor Kirkland will do anything to get the child back," Reed said tersely. "You may not know that I have represented the Mayfields for thirty years and I was the attorney in the first custody case. I've gone up against this young man before, I've seen him operate, and I have nothing but admiration for his ... persuasive abilities."

Carol said nothing.

"Kirkland is good-looking and charming, the perfect con man. I am personal friends with the Mayfields, as well as their attorney, and I watched Kirkland manipulate and seduce Alice Mayfield until she forgot everything her parents had taught her. She was a sheltered, unsophisticated child, educated in girls' schools, totally unequipped to handle a huckster like Kirkland. She rejected her parents for him and finally broke their hearts."

Carol wrested her arm from his viselike grasp. "Goodbye, Mr. Reed."

"I assume that you know Kirkland's interest in the girl goes beyond fatherly concern?" Reed said, firing a parting shot.

Carol stared at him.

"Alicia is wealthy. She has an indissoluble trust fund from her grandmother, the principal of which will be delivered to her when she is eighteen. Her custodial parent controls that fund until she comes of age and receives the income from the trust."

"Tay has enough money."

"Ah, Miss Lansing, you are naive. No one ever has enough money, and my recollection is that Taylor Kirkland has been trying to escape his financially unsound background since he was old enough to add a column of figures."

"Through hard work!" Carol shot back at him, more shaken by this revelation than she wanted him to see.

"Through women," Reed replied sadly, satisfied that he had finally scored a point. "First Alice Mayfield, now you and his only child."

"I'm not going to continue this conversation, Mr. Reed. The hearing is set for October third, I will see you then."

"Think about what I've said, Miss Lansing," Reed called after her as she left the conference room.

Carol returned to her cubbyhole, staring down at a page of notes until the elevator closed behind Reed. Then she tried to concentrate on her work once more, but she found Reed's words coming back to haunt her.

She believed in Tay, she really did, but why hadn't he told her about Alicia's money? Was it just an oversight? And it was certainly true that Carol had helped him immeasurably in launching his renewed custody battle, she had done little else but work on it with him for the past couple of months. She knew that it was Reed's job to look for the weak spots on the opposing team and attack them, and his visit was an indication that he was worried about the way the case was shaping up for the Mayfields, but she still couldn't shake a sense of nagging unease. She had no complaints about Tay's physical passion or his kindness toward her, but he had never said in so many words that he loved her. Did words matter so much? Or couldn't he bring himself to make the declaration because he really was using her? Could a con man have such a delicate conscience in that regard? Carol's head spun with all the unanswered questions.

The phone was ringing as she let herself into her studio apartment. She walked through the living room, dropping her purse and briefcase on the sofa, then picked up the phone.

"Hello?" she said, leaning against the half wall that separated the galley kitchen from the other room.

"Carol, it's John Spencer," a masculine voice said.

"Oh, hi, John. How are you?"

"How are you, Carol? I haven't heard a word from you since you moved back to New York."

"I'm sorry, I've been so busy..."

"Yes, I've heard. Congratulations on your engagement."

"I guess you were pretty surprised when you heard about Tay and me," Carol said sheepishly.

"Not as surprised as you think. Even when you were at each other's throats it was obvious that the sparks were flying."

Carol laughed.

"Carol, I'm sorry to interrupt a happy time with bad news, but I've heard from Gloria Ashland and she does plan to sue for the profits from the sale of the Strathmere house. Apparently she can produce witnesses who will testify that your father planned to leave it to her."

Carol sighed heavily. Just what she needed at this point, her father's inamorata to resurface with her hand out.

"Tell her she can have whatever's left after the liens are settled," Carol said.

"Are you sure?" John asked in a concerned tone. "Her case is doubtful at best, there's no provision in the will, no written addendum. If you go to court you stand a strong chance of getting rid of her for good."

"Just tell her she can have the money. That will get rid of her. One court case at a time is all I can stand."

"What do you mean?"

"Tay is refiling for custody of his little girl."

"Oh, yes, I remember hearing something about that recently," John said.

"He lost custody of the child to his in-laws after his wife was killed."

"His wife came from money, as I recall."

"Yes."

"Has anything changed that might alter the outcome this time?" John asked.

"Tay's business is established, and we'll be married. Alicia will have two parents."

"That might make the in-laws all the more determined to keep her. They won't want to see anyone replacing their daughter in the little girl's life."

"I know."

There was a long silence on John's end of the line, and then the lawyer said, "All this with Kirkland happened pretty fast, didn't it, Carol?"

"Yes, I guess so."

"Are you sure of what you're doing?"

Carol's heart sank. She could hear in Spencer's tone that he had sized up the situation and was questioning it, but was much too nice to say so.

"I don't know, John," she said honestly. "I'm in love."

"It sounds like it might be a nasty court battle for Kirkland's kid," Spencer said. "And even if Kirkland wins, instant families are often hard to handle. It could be a tough adjustment for the child."

"That's why I don't want to bother with Gloria. Just do whatever it takes to make her disappear."

"All right. I'll be in touch about the final arrangements. And Carol?"

"Yes?"

"Don't worry too much about what I just said. I feel like I'm standing in for your father sometimes and maybe I said too much. If you're in love, take the chance. You don't get anywhere in life if you don't take a chance."

Carol stared down at her shoes. Her father had been in love, he had taken a chance. What had it gotten him? Gloria.

"Carol, are you still there?"

"Yes, I am. Thanks, John. Let me know what happens with Gloria."

Carol hung up the phone before John could prolong the conversation. She looked at the clock, wanting to call Tay, but he was out on a job and wouldn't be back in his office until six. She would just have to wait.

Carol kicked off her shoes and was heading toward her tiny bathroom to take a shower when her doorbell sounded. She was planning to ignore it when Jane's voice came from the hall.

"Carol, open up, it's me."

Carol padded to the door and undid the locks to admit her friend.

"Hi," Jane said, charging past her to dump a large paper bag on the dining area table. "I got the chili, but Gristede's was out of the sesame rolls you like..." She stopped talking when she registered Carol's blank stare.

"Did you make other plans?" Jane said. "Is Tay about to arrive?"

"No, he's working, I won't see him until tomorrow. I just had a rotten day and my feet hurt and my father's tootsie wants more money and—"

"So, sit down. I'll do everything. What's up with Grasping Gloria?"

"Oh, she just wants the profits from the Strathmere house, but that's not the worst of it."

"So what's the worst of it? I must say that you look extremely unfestive for a young lady who's engaged to the cutest guy on the Atlantic seaboard."

"I had a visitor today."

"The prince of darkness?" Jane suggested, removing a plastic container from the bag she'd brought.

"Just about. The Mayfields' lawyer."

"And what did he do to put you in this gloriously transcendent mood?"

"He suggested, rather strongly, that Tay was using me in order to get Alicia back."

"Come on, Carol, you know the opposition will say anything during the pretrial period in order to shake you up. He must be fishing to come and see you in person that way. What exactly did he say?"

"He reminded me of what I already knew. That I had set up Tay's case, gotten him his lawyer, enabled him to present the picture of a stable home. And he gave me a further piece of news. Tay's daughter is worth millions, and the custodial parent manages the money until the child is of age."

"Tay never told you that?" Jane asked, pausing in the act of opening a cabinet.

"No."

"But you must have known that some provision would be made for a kid coming from that sort of background."

"I know it sounds stupid now, but I never even thought about it. I just accepted Tay's story of a father unjustly separated from his child."

"And now you're questioning it?"

Carol shrugged. "This lawyer who came to see me was so convincing...."

"That's why they pay him the big bucks," Jane said.

"And it bothers me that I've never even seen Tay's little girl. He had her with him for two weeks before we met, but once he filed the papers, the Mayfields petitioned the court to suspend his visitation rights until the dispute was settled. He hasn't had her for even a day since then. I mean, what if she hates me on sight?"

"Carol, nobody hates you on sight."

"She may think I'm replacing her mother."

"If she was two when Alice died, she won't even remember her mother, which is a shame in itself, but better for you."

"God knows what the Mayfields are telling her." Carol sighed. "They're probably painting me as the Whore of Babylon."

"Most likely they're telling her nothing at all in the hope they won't lose her."

"I don't know. I was so sure for so long, and now suddenly I'm all confused. Maybe it is better for her to stay in the home she's had for the last five years, but the fact remains that Tay's own child was taken from him...." Her voice trailed off into silence.

"You need a medicinal dose of your beloved," Jane said briskly, turning on the oven. "When you see him tomorrow, all your doubts will vanish. Now if you can manage to get your feeble self out of that chair, I would like a drink. The cook's pump must be primed. Do you have any Scotch?"

"I think Tay left some here." Carol rose to get the bottle, her mind still on her troubles.

Jane left to return to the Jersey shore in the morning. Carol spent the day doing laundry and straightening her apartment, tending to the chores she didn't have time for during the week. When she looked at the clock and saw that Tay was due in an hour, she hurried to shower and change. She was pouring him a drink when he came through the door.

Jane was right. One look at him and all of Carol's doubts vanished. He opened his arms and she ran into them.

"Boy, did I miss you," he said against her hair, dropping the bouquet he held onto a table. He tilted her head back and kissed her, steering her toward the bedroom. They left a trail of clothing in the hall and wound up making love on the rug.

"Are you hungry?" Carol said dreamily afterward, snuggling into his shoulder. "Jane made enough chili last night to feed an army, there's plenty of it left in the fridge."

"I don't think I can move right now. Maybe later," he replied, stroking her bare arm as he looked around the closet-size bedroom. "How can you live here?" he asked. "This place is like a telephone booth."

"It's all I could afford as a law student, and it's close to the school. I used to have a roommate to share expenses."

"You don't need a roommate. You've already got the glue sniffers on the corner and the bag lady in the stairwell."

"Not fond of New York?" Carol asked teasingly.

"I can't wait until you're living with me," he replied. He closed his eyes.

"I had a visitor yesterday afternoon," Carol began casually, before he could fall asleep, noticing the pack of cigarettes peeking out of the pocket of his discarded pants. He was still smoking.

"Yeah?" he replied, his eyes still closed.

"Bartholomew Reed."

His eyes shot open. "The Mayfields' lawyer?"

"The very same."

Tay sat up and looked at her. "That guy's a shark. What did he want?"

"To feel me out, see what we were planning."

"Isn't that unethical or something?"

"What, for lawyers to talk before a hearing?"

"Right."

"No, it's just unwise to reveal too much to the opposition, but I didn't tell him anything he didn't already know."

"I'll bet he told you a few things," Tay said darkly, reaching around on the floor for his pants. He extracted a cigarette from the pack and lit it.

"Like what?" Carol said.

"The party line from the last custody hearing—that I'm some sort of jaded gigolo who led that poor little innocent Alice Mayfield astray."

"Yes, he tried to give me that impression."

"It isn't true, Carol. Alice and I just fell in love, like kids do all the time. The fact that her parents had money was incidental, not the reason I wanted her."

"And Alicia?" Carol asked, hating herself but determined to raise the issue.

"What about her?"

"She has a trust fund."

"So? I told you that."

"No, you didn't."

"I didn't? I thought I had, or maybe I assumed that you'd realize she would."

"Reed says that her custodial parent manages the money until she reaches majority."

Tay exhaled a plume of smoke and then looked over at her, his eyes narrowing.

"Oh, I see," he said quietly. "I'm the greedy daddy who wants to get his mitts on the kiddie in order to get his mitts on the money. And I've duped you into helping me, just like I duped Alicia's mother. Is that about the size of it?"

"Yes," Carol responded, not meeting his gaze.

"And you listened to this?"

"I had no choice, Tay. He cornered me in the conference room and—"

"What?" Tay demanded. "Tied you to a chair? You must have provided a willing ear, it seems like you got quite a bit of information."

"He was trying to rattle me, Tay."

Tay snorted bitterly, standing abruptly. "He did a very good job. You're looking at me like I'm a suspect in a lineup." He retrieved his pants and put them on, jamming his legs into them and then putting his hands in his pockets. His left hand came out with something in it, and Carol drew back as a small box whizzed toward her and landed in her lap.

"I forgot I had that," he said, not looking at her. "I was feeling guilty about all of this, getting you caught up in my problems and not giving you a proper engagement ring or anything, so there it is."

Carol opened the box and saw a beautiful marquise diamond set in gold and displayed against a bed of midnight-blue velvet.

"I hope you like it. I never bought one for Alice, so I didn't have any guide."

"Oh, Tay," she whispered, dropping the box and crawling across the rug to fling herself on him. "I'm sorry. I shouldn't have listened to Reed, I should have thrown him out when he arrived."

He clutched at her, his bare arms tightening around her.

"Can you forgive me?" she asked.

He didn't answer, and when Carol looked up at his face she saw that there were tears in his eyes.

"You have to believe in me," he said, his voice catching in his throat as she rested her head on his shoulder.

"If you don't believe in me, no one else will, don't you see that?"

"I see that. I am so sorry."

"Everything will be all right if you just stick with me and don't lose faith. I know Reed is good, he beat me once already, but this time the outcome will be different. I'll get Alicia back, we'll be together, and the lonely past will be like a bad dream. For both of us."

Carol raised her head to kiss him, and he pulled her down onto the bed.

The following Saturday, Carol drove down to Strathmere to see the real estate agent handling the sale of her father's house. There were several prospective buyers, including one who wanted to pay cash, which would eliminate the wait for mortgage approval. His offer was lower than the other bids, however, so Carol had a decision to make. Even though Gloria might wind up with the profits, Carol didn't want to give the house away.

After her business discussion, she went to Tay's apartment, where she found a note telling her that he would be home around four. She busied herself dusting and straightening the rooms until she heard a knock at the door. She glanced at the clock and saw that it was just past three. Maybe Tay was early, but why was he knocking on his own door? She went to answer the summons, dropping her dust rag on the kitchen table as she passed.

The door opened to reveal a little girl of seven or eight standing on the small porch at the top of the stairs. Her hair was blond, her eyes were blue, and she looked like a china doll replica of Tay.

"Who are you?" she demanded of Carol. "Where's my daddy?"

Nine

Carol was so startled that she didn't know how to respond for several seconds. Then she said, "You must be Alicia! It's so nice to meet you. My name is Carol. I'm...a friend of your father's. Why don't you come inside and we'll call him."

"Where is he?" Alicia asked, following Carol through the door. She was dressed in blue jeans and a pink Izod sweater. Her hair was pulled back with barrettes and she clutched a small overnight bag in one hand.

"He's at work. I'm going to phone his office right now." Carol picked up the receiver, took a breath, and asked carefully, "Do your grandparents know that you're here?"

"No," the child said, wrinkling her nose. "They sent me to a stinky camp and I didn't like it. I had to do chores there and I couldn't ride Falfa and all they served for dinner was spaghetti with some yucky orange sauce. So I left and came here to see Dad.''

Carol paused in the act of dialing. ''Did you tell anyone you were leaving?'' Carol asked in a strained voice.

Alicia shrugged. ''If I had reached Grandma she would have made me stay and if I had told Miss Lisa she would have just given me a talk about sharing and pitching in and all that stuff she always says. So I called Grandpa's driver from Miss Lisa's office when no one was in there and he brought me here.''

Carol closed her eyes, picturing hysterical camp counselors and all-points bulletins and the outraged Mayfields suing everybody. She finished dialing Tay's office, learned that he was still out on a site, and dialed him on the mobile phone. When Mike answered, she waited for him to get Tay, tapping her foot, until she heard Tay say, ''Carol?''

''Tay, you'd better come home right now. Alicia is here.''

There was a moment of stunned silence and then he said, ''There? At the house?''

''You got it. Apparently the Mayfields sent her to some summer camp and she ran away from it. They must be going wild at Camp Whatchamacallit, thinking she's been kidnapped or worse.''

Tay muttered something under his breath and then asked, ''Is she all right?''

''She seems to be fine. She apparently got the Mayfields' chauffeur to drive her from wherever it was to Strathmere. I can't wait for the Mayfields to hear that bulletin. I hope the poor man has unemployment insurance.''

''Let me talk to her,'' Tay said grimly.

"Your father wants to speak to you," Carol said, handing Alicia the receiver.

The child grinned and grabbed the phone. "Daddy!" she said delightedly.

Carol couldn't hear what Tay was saying, but the little girl's smile faded and then disappeared. She listened in silence and then protested, "But they went on vacation and didn't take me! They were going to Hawaii to see the volcanos and the pineapples and the hula dancers and they sent me to Camp Yucky Sauce instead!"

There was another silence, during which Alicia's lower lip protruded and her chin began to tremble. She finally handed Carol the phone and said in a tiny voice, "Daddy's mad at me."

"Tay?" Carol said into the receiver.

She was answered with a sigh. "You'd better call that camp and tell them she's okay," he said wearily.

"Where is it?"

"I told Alicia to give you the information. She will."

"She looks a little shaky, Tay," Carol whispered into the phone, watching the child anxiously. Alicia had gone into the living room and was playing with the TV remote, a single tear sliding down a porcelain cheek.

"She should, after the talking to I just gave her. Can you imagine that little bit of nothing calling a chauffeur to take her to the Jersey shore? I wonder who taught her that trick? The high-and-mighty Mayfields, that's who. And what kind of a driver picks up a minor child from a summer camp and just drives away without his employer's authorization?"

"The kind who can't reach his vacationing boss and has to make a quick decision," Carol replied. "It was a tough call, Tay. He probably takes orders from your daughter every day. If he refused Alicia and forced her to find alternative transportation he might have been in bigger trouble. At least this way he knows where she went.''

"They pack her off to a camp instead of giving her some time and taking her on their vacation,'' Tay said, fuming. "I'd like to knock the exalted Mayfield heads together.''

"Alicia must be very smart, Tay, to pull something like this off by herself.''

"She is smart, but just at this moment I wish she weren't. Look, try to keep a lid on things there and I'll be home in twenty minutes.''

"All right,'' Carol said.

"And don't forget to call that camp.''

"I'll call.'' Carol hung up the phone and went in to Alicia, who was sitting on the edge of the sofa, staring sightlessly at a talk show.

"Alicia, I need to know the name and location of the camp so I can call the people there and tell them you're all right,'' Carol said.

The child turned a miserable face to Carol and said, "Camp Tekawitha in Lake Hopatcong. It's in Morris County. My counselor's Miss Lisa. I don't know her last name.''

"That's fine, Alicia. You just wait here and I'll be right back.'' Carol made the call and spoke to a relieved Miss Lisa, who was so thrilled to hear that Alicia was safe in her father's house that she didn't even mention the Mayfields. Carol gently reminded her that the grandparents had custody, and Miss Lisa quickly volunteered to call them at the Halekulani Hotel at Waikiki and inform them of the situation. If they were unavailable, she would leave a message.

Carol hung up thoughtfully, wondering if they would return from their trip immediately or leave Tay to deal with the problem.

Carol went back to Alicia, who was now curled up on the sofa, tracing the seam of a seat cushion.

Carol shut off the television and sat next to the child.

"Daddy is really mad at me," Alicia said, looking up, fresh tears welling in her eyes.

"He was just scared, Alicia. Adults get angry when they're scared, especially once the fright is over and the reaction sets in. He was just thinking of all the bad things that might have happened to you on the way here."

"My daddy's not scared of anything," Alicia said proudly, wiping her nose on her forearm.

Carol got up and handed her a tissue from the box on the coffee table.

"He was scared of something harming his child. All daddies are."

Alicia blew her nose and said worriedly, "Will he still be mad when he gets here?"

"Even if he is, he'll soon remember that he loves you, I guarantee it. But you must promise him never to do anything like this again."

"Even if I have to go back to Camp Yucky Sauce?" Alicia asked worriedly.

"I'm fairly sure you won't have to go back there," Carol said, casting about in her mind for something to distract the child. "Now let me see. Are you hungry?"

Alicia brightened, nodding.

"What would you like?" Carol asked, trying to remember what was in Tay's perennially understocked kitchen. "Some fruit, or a sandwich?"

"Have you got any Hi-Hos?" Alicia asked hopefully.

"I doubt it," Carol said. "I'm sure I can find something."

She returned to the living room a few minutes later with some grapes, an apple, and a stack of graham crackers. Alicia looked disappointed, but began dutifully to eat.

"Are you my father's girlfriend?" she suddenly asked Carol, looking at her over the rim of the apple with Tay's azure eyes.

Carol froze in the act of plumping a sofa cushion. "I . . . uh, yes," Carol finally said carefully.

"Are you going to marry him?" Alicia demanded.

Carol hesitated. "I think you should talk to your dad about this," she then said firmly, unwilling to negotiate this mine field without Tay.

Alicia shrugged. "I knew someday I would get a new mother," she said.

"You only have one mother, Alicia, and I know she loved you very much. If I become your stepmother I hope we will be great friends, but I won't take your mother's place. No one could do that."

"I don't remember her," Alicia said softly.

"I know. But your father does, and he tells you about her, doesn't he?"

"It's not the same," Alicia said sadly.

Carol was silent. She could not disagree with that.

"Would I have to call you mom?" Alicia asked.

"You can call me whatever you like," Carol replied mildly.

That seemed to satisfy the child, and she was popping the last of the grapes into her mouth as Tay came through the door.

"Daddy!" Alicia said, jumping up joyfully, her anxieties forgotten.

Tay held out his arms and Alicia ran into them. He lifted the child into the air and swung her around before setting her back down and embracing her.

Carol felt tears spring into her eyes as she watched them. She waited until Tay looked up at her and then said to him, "You two obviously have a few things to discuss. I'll go into the bedroom and read so you can have some time alone."

Tay shot her a grateful glance over Alicia's shoulder as she went into the other room and closed the door.

Carol sat on the bed and tried to read one of Tay's architectural magazines, but her attention wandered. She couldn't help but wonder what implications Alicia's flight from summer camp held for Tay's upcoming custody hearing. When the phone rang a short time later she heard Tay answer it in the other room, then went back to her article on federal-style brick buildings in Bucks County, Pennsylvania. Ten minutes later Tay knocked on the door.

"Yes?" she called.

He opened the door.

"Everything okay?" Carol asked.

He nodded. "Alicia and I have had a meeting of the minds and have decided to go out and get some ice cream. Would you like to join us?"

Carol slid off the bed and followed him into the kitchen, where Alicia was sitting on one of the straight-back chairs, swinging her legs. There were traces of tears on her face, but she looked serene. The storm had obviously passed.

They walked down to Hepworth's, Strathmere's only drugstore, featuring a forties-style soda fountain that actually dated from the forties. While Alicia spun around on the leather-topped stool, waiting for her banana split,

Carol and Tay sat at one of the small wrought-iron tables nearby.

"How did it go?" Carol asked in a low tone.

"I think it went all right. It's difficult to make her understand that she can't do anything that comes into her head at any time, because the Mayfields are so permissive," he said in a resigned tone.

"What was the phone call about?"

"The phone call was from Chester Mayfield's secretary, informing me that the Mayfields won't cut short their trip. Their car will come for Alicia on Tuesday." He shook his head. "If things keep on this way, I don't know what will become of that kid."

"I can tell she's a nice little girl, Tay, despite this episode."

"She could be a nice little girl. They're spoiling her rotten, Carol. She's basically a sweet, good-natured kid, but they're turning her into a perfect snob. She ran way from that camp because the counsellors were asking her to do chores, like that was the end of the world! Oh, and she couldn't ride her pony, let's not forget that." He shook his head. "I have to get her away from them." His jaw set with determination.

Carol looked over at Alicia, who was making a tent of toothpicks while she waited for her banana split.

"It may be crass to bring this up right now, Tay, but there is an up side to this whole experience," Carol said quietly.

"And what could that possibly be?" Tay asked, looking at her as if she were deranged.

"From a legal point of view, the Mayfields stashing Alicia in the camp while they went their merry way on a separate vacation might be construed as neglect. Insensitivity, at the very least."

"Don't wealthy parents do that sort of thing all the time?" Tay asked.

"Not when they have a custody battle looming," Carol replied dryly. "The Mayfields couldn't have checked with Reed before doing such a thing, or else they must be just as arrogant as you said. Alicia was obviously unhappy with their decision or she wouldn't have run away. And they aren't cutting short their trip to come home and deal with the situation. Doesn't that show a lack of concern? Smyth can make a big deal of this, and the judge could very well listen."

"I suppose you're right," Tay said thoughtfully.

"And why not?" Carol went on. "Evidence of their conduct and your daughter's state of mind are relevant. You didn't cause this incident, but you can certainly use it to your advantage."

Alicia received her dessert and headed toward their table, carefully balancing the stainless-steel boat that contained several lumps of ice cream topped with different shades of goop.

"We'll continue this later," Tay said to Carol in an undertone, and then called out to Alicia, "Think you've got enough calories there, kiddo?"

After dinner that night Carol departed for the XCel Motel, explaining to Tay that her staying overnight in the apartment while Alicia was present was unwise; the Mayfields' lawyer could distort such a situation very easily when presenting it in court. On Sunday, Tay and Carol took Alicia to the Ocean City Zoo, and by the time they returned to Tay's apartment that evening Carol had to leave to drive back to Manhattan.

"Goodbye, Alicia," Carol said, bending to put herself on the child's eye level. "Even if it began badly, I'm happy we had this chance to spend some time together."

Alicia extended her hand to shake Carol's, then thought better of it and leaned forward to kiss Carol's cheek.

Carol looked at Tay, who winked at her.

"Will we go to the zoo again?" Alicia asked tremulously.

"I'm sure we can arrange that," Carol said.

"Go inside for a minute, honey, I want to talk to Carol before she leaves," Tay said to the child.

Alicia waved goodbye to Carol, her expression grave, then went into the living room.

"I'll get her back," Tay said fiercely, looking after the little girl. "I have to."

Carol embraced him, and his arms came around her tightly.

"Every time that long black car comes for her, and she disappears into the back of it, looking so small and lost, a little piece of me goes away with her," he said.

"You don't have much longer to wait," Carol said. "And I think you have a very good chance."

He pulled back to look at her. "You're not just saying that to reassure me?" he asked.

"No. I think you have a very good chance."

He kissed her quickly on the lips. "Go," he said. "Call me in the morning."

"I will."

Carol ran down the steps and then waved at him from the bottom.

He saluted, then went through the door and closed it.

The day of the hearing approached, and Carol worked feverishly with Harold Smyth to prepare for it. The file was growing thicker every minute as they collected affidavits and supporting documents. Tay hovered, overseeing Carol's efforts anxiously, aware that their future would be determined by the outcome of the proceeding. He smoked more and talked less, and Carol tried to be supportive, but she was feeling the pressure herself. He was depending on her to get his child back for him, and despite the positive picture she presented to him, she wasn't sure she could do it.

By the time they finally sat in the hearing room, waiting for the judge to enter, Tay had retreated into almost total silence. Carol reached for his hand; it was cold. She looked over at the opposition's table and saw Bartholomew Reed, every strand of his leonine hair in place, his face impassive. He didn't look at her.

The Mayfields sat in the first row behind the lawyers' table. Regina Mayfield was a well-preserved, frosted blonde in her fifties, impeccably dressed in a light wool suit, whose understated makeup and tasteful jewelry reflected the money spent to achieve the effect. Her stocky husband sat at her side, staring straight ahead, his features set.

They looked as if they meant business.

Alicia was not present. The judge had already ruled that she was too young to be questioned or to offer an opinion on where she would like to live.

The judge, a stout, sixtyish woman named Hanson with a penetrating gaze, entered the courtroom. They all rose as the clerk commanded them to, and the hearing began.

The proceeding droned on in standard fashion as the documents were entered into the record and the witnesses called. Carol made notes on the pad in front of her as the Mayfields testified, and then various friends and servants of the Mayfields testified about what wonderful parents they were and how happy the child was in their care. Then Smyth presented Tay's case, leaning heavily on the recent episode of Alicia's flight from camp to show the child's unhappiness, and suggesting that the Mayfields' continuing their vacation in spite of it demonstrated their lack of concern. Reed countered by saying that the child was playing the adults off against each other, as many children in such situations do, and the Mayfields were generous in allowing the child extra time with her father while they were away. Finally the lawyers were invited to question the participants for the benefit of the judge. Tay acquitted himself well when questioned, not rising to the bait Reed offered on several occasions and keeping his temper under control. Carol was proud of him.

Reed interviewed several other people and then looked at Carol for the first time. She was accustomed to such proceedings, but she still jumped when her name was called by the clerk. Praying that she would be a good witness, she rose and walked to the front of the courtroom, taking her seat in the box. During her legal training she had often done the questioning, but being on the other end of the interaction was a new experience.

She was sworn in and Reed began his interrogation slowly, asking for general information about her background and education. It wasn't clear where he was going until he asked suddenly, "And did you enjoy a sexual relationship with Mr. Kirkland prior to your becoming engaged to him, Miss Lansing?"

Carol's eyes met Tay's across the room, then she looked at Smyth, but he did not object.

"Yes," she replied.

"And how many other sexual relationships have you enjoyed in the past?" Reed asked.

Now Smyth rose to his feet. "Your Honor, I object. Miss Lansing's past sexual history is not at all relevant to this proceeding."

Judge Hanson looked at Reed, who raised his brows.

"I disagree, Your Honor," Reed said. "If Mr. Kirkland regains custody of the minor child, Miss Lansing will be the mother figure in the family. Her character is certainly an issue since she will be marrying the child's father in the future."

"All right, Mr. Reed," the judge said, "you may pursue this line of questioning. But I warn you, proceed with caution."

Carol steeled herself for what was to come. It was clear that Reed thought he could make some headway with her, and he was prepared to try.

"Should I repeat the question, Miss Lansing?" Reed asked smoothly.

"I remember the question. I had two lovers before Mr. Kirkland, one in college and one in law school."

"And don't you find such promiscuity unwise in this day and age?" Reed asked.

This time Smyth leapt to his feet. "Your Honor, this is outrageous. To characterize taking three lovers over a lifespan of twenty-five years as promiscuity is patently absurd. Miss Lansing should not have to answer that question."

The judge leaned forward to address the Mayfield attorney. "I agree. Mr. Reed, I did warn you."

"Your Honor, Miss Lansing's judgment is an issue here," Reed protested.

"Rephrase the question or withdraw it," Hanson barked, sitting back in her chair.

Reed sighed. "I'll withdraw it. Miss Lansing, you are currently involved in a property dispute with a Miss Gloria Ashland, is that correct?"

Carol was momentarily startled. Reed's detectives must really be good if they had unearthed Gloria. Carol took a few seconds to compose herself and then said, "That is not correct."

"Really?" Reed said, his eyes narrowing. "I remind you that you are under oath, Miss Lansing."

"Your Honor, please," Smyth said wearily, not even bothering to get up.

"I'll do the reminding, Mr. Reed," the judge said. "The witness will answer the question."

"I have already instructed my lawyer, Mr. John Spencer, of Avalon, to give Miss Ashland whatever she wants. There is no dispute," Carol said.

"So you deny that you were ever involved in a conflict with Miss Ashland over the settlement of your father's estate?" Reed snapped, annoyed that Carol had neatly sidestepped the issue.

Smyth was on his feet again. "Your honor, Mr. Reed is clearly fishing, and fishing hard, for some shred of evidence to discredit Miss Lansing. Whatever the particulars regarding Miss Lansing's late father's estate, they are not relevant to this proceeding."

"They're relevant, Your Honor," Reed said.

The judge looked at him. "Where are you going with this, Mr. Reed?"

"I am seeking to establish a pattern of avaricious conduct. Since the child involved is a wealthy one, Miss Lansing's motive in marrying the child's father and thus becoming a surrogate parent to the child might not be entirely altruistic."

"Don't you think you're reaching just a bit, Mr. Reed?" Judge Hanson asked, raising one penciled brow.

"If Your Honor will allow me to proceed, the relevance of this line of inquiry will become clear," Reed said.

The judge nodded resignedly, and Reed continued to grill Carol about Gloria's past claims on the Lansing property until Smyth finally rose to his feet and said, "Your Honor, this is getting us nowhere. The only thing Mr. Reed has established with this line of questioning is that Miss Lansing has been exercising her right to defend her inheritance against the rather dubious claims of her father's companion, who was never married to him. Miss Lansing's eagerness to settle those claims and get on with her life hardly bespeaks an 'avaricious' nature determined to claim every penny."

The judge nodded. "I agree with Mr. Smyth, I think we have had enough of this. Unless you have something new to introduce, Mr. Reed, I suggest you wrap this up, dismiss Miss Lansing, and move on to other issues."

Carol breathed a sigh of relief, and when she looked at Tay, he gave her the thumb's-up sign. Seconds later she was climbing down from the witness stand and joining him.

"Well done," he said, leaning in to press his mouth to her ear. "They've got nothing, and Reed only succeeded in making that clear. You were terrific."

The formalities droned on for some time longer, taking up most of the morning, and at the end of the session the judge said that she would be issuing her decision within a week. The Mayfields and their attorney rose as one body and left the courtroom, making eye contact with no one.

"They didn't even look at you," Carol said to Tay.

A uniformed driver waiting at the door took Reed's briefcase. He then led the little procession out to the limousine Carol had seen idling at the curb on her way in that day.

"They never do," he said, shrugging.

"But you were married to their daughter. You're the father of their grandchild."

"I'm an unfortunate accident, a problem they can't solve with money. They can't make me go away, but they can ignore me while they're forced to deal with the inconveniences I create."

Harold Smyth closed his briefcase and came over to shake Tay's hand.

"How do you think it went?" Tay asked anxiously.

"It went very well for you, it couldn't have gone better, as I'm sure you know. But we're not out of the woods yet. If the judge thinks that the child's accustomed living circumstances shouldn't be disturbed, she could still rule against you. The case law goes either way on that issue, it's really a crapshoot."

Tay nodded, his expression thoughtful.

Smyth clapped him on the shoulder. "Try to take it easy while you're waiting, it's out of our hands now. And I hope you appreciate how much this little lady here has done for you. She worked like a field hand researching the case record for situations like yours in which the child had been returned to the natural parent."

Tay looked at Carol. "I appreciate her more than I can say," Tay replied softly.

Smyth glanced at his watch. "I have to go. Kirkland, I'll be in touch, and Carol, I'll see you at the office." He winked at her.

Carol nodded.

"Nice guy," Tay commented, looking after Smyth as he walked out of the room.

"If you can afford him," Carol replied, and Tay grinned.

"It's going to be a long wait until we get the ruling," Carol said to him.

He nodded soberly.

"In the meantime, can we have lunch? I'm starving."

"I think we can arrange that." Tay put his arm around Carol and led her out of the room.

It was ten days before the judge ruled on the custody case. Carol was working at her desk when Harold Smyth stuck his head into her cubbyhole, a wide smile on his face.

"We won," Carol whispered when she saw the court papers he was holding.

Smyth nodded. "Custody has been restored to the father," Smyth said. "The Mayfields have some visitation rights, of course. You can read all the details, but the upshot is that Kirkland gets the little girl back."

"Are you going to call him?" Carol asked.

Smyth smiled again. "I think you should do it, don't you?"

Carol dialed the phone, finding the numbers on the pad through a film of tears. When she reached Tay's office and heard that he was out on a job, she had to restrain herself from biting Madeline's head off in frustration. She dialed the number of the mobile phone with a shaky finger, her impatience mounting further as it was answered by Mike, Tay's crew chief.

"He's up on the roof, Carol," Mike said. "Can I give him a message?"

"Please get him, Mike. This is important."

"Okay." Carol heard the background noise of motors and men's shouting voices until Tay finally came on the line.

"Carol?" he said.

"You won," she replied. "Alicia is yours."

Carol could have heard the whoop he let out without the assistance of the telephone.

"You did it," she said.

"*We* did it."

"You have to talk to Smyth about the details of transferring custody and so on, but the ruling was issued today."

"I'll pick you up at eight and we'll go to that little place around the corner from your apartment," Tay said. "This calls for a major celebration."

"You're going to drive over here from Jersey tonight?"

"Of course I am. I have to be with you, Carol. We have to make plans."

"Okay. I'll see you tonight."

She could hear him calling the good news to Mike as he hung up the phone.

That night at dinner Tay was bursting with plans about their new life with Alicia and what the three of them would do as a family. Carol knew that the adjustment would be difficult for the little girl, but she couldn't bring herself to dim Tay's happiness over his victory by injecting a note of harsh reality. It would intrude on its own, and they would have to deal with it when it did.

Alicia would be turned over to Tay by a court-appointed social worker in a few days. Carol agreed that it would be best for Tay to pick up the little girl alone; there would be time enough to reintroduce Carol when the child had adjusted to her new situation. Tay said he would call Carol after Alicia had settled in at his place. They parted that night with high hopes for the future.

Several days went by, and Carol didn't hear from Tay. He was usually faithful about staying in touch, but she didn't become alarmed until Friday arrived and he hadn't called her back. She left several messages at his office and he wasn't answering his home phone. Finally, at the weekend, she took her father's car from the garage and drove to Strathmere.

In Tay's office she found Madeline, who told her that Tay had gone away for a few days. But Mike was lurking in the background, looking uncomfortable. When Madeline stepped out, Carol cornered Mike and asked him what was going on.

Mike's face reddened; he didn't like being caught in the middle of a sticky situation.

"I think it's going to be longer than a few days, Carol," Mike said unhappily. "He left me in charge of the business and gave me check-signing privileges. I'm supposed to deposit all the payments and complete the current jobs, but he told me not to take on any new work."

"When did he tell you this?"

"Tuesday? Yeah, Tuesday."

"Did he say where he was going?"

"No. You mean he didn't call you?" Mike was in an agony of embarrassment, but Carol didn't even answer him. She ran out of the office and up the flight of stairs to Tay's apartment, letting herself in with her key.

It was obvious that the rooms hadn't been occupied in several days. There were no cups in the sink, no discarded garments strewn about the furniture. When Carol went into the bedroom she already knew what she would find.

The closet was empty.

Tay was gone.

Ten

"All I can tell you is that there must be some logical explanation," Jane observed, watching the snow fall past the windows of Carol's apartment.

"Of course there is," Carol answered. "Tay ditched me."

"He was in love with you, Carol. Men are my hobby, and I know all the signs."

"He was just a good actor. He used me to get his daughter and then cleaned out his bank account to skip town with her."

"He asked you to marry him!"

"So much the better for his plan if I had. It would have looked even prettier to the judge, and a marriage license would not have stopped him from taking off, you know that. How many desertion cases have you filed?"

"I just can't believe it," Jane muttered.

"It's taken me almost three months, but I'm beginning to," Carol replied miserably.

"I don't suppose the Mayfields know anything," Jane said, casting a sidelong glance at her friend.

"Do you think they would tell me if they did? They regard me as Tay's cohort in crime, an architect of this disaster. I've tried calling them. Bartholomew Reed left a message with Harold Smyth saying that if I continued to 'harass' his clients he would pursue a legal remedy against me. They've probably got a battalion of investigators on the case. I'm sure they're frantic to get Alicia back, but they don't know where she is."

"Are you positive?"

Carol nodded. "Harold told me that he heard they've petitioned several times for classified police documents. They're in the dark, too."

"How are things going at the office?" Jane asked.

Carol rolled her eyes. "Thank God we got that murder case last week. Now they have something else to talk about besides my tragic history with Taylor Kirkland."

"And the urbane Mr. Smyth?"

"Well, he's stopped looking at me as if I'm about to have hysterics every minute," Carol replied dryly.

"Maybe he was just worried about his bill being paid," Jane observed.

"It was paid. Tay told Mike to pay it. It may have been my erstwhile fiancé's last official act before he disappeared."

"It must be awful having everyone know what happened," Jane said sympathetically. "At work, I mean."

"I've had my fill of pitying looks."

"And Mike knows nothing?"

"He says he doesn't."

"Do you believe him?"

Carol sighed, then nodded. "I think Tay just told him to handle the business and then took off. But you can't imagine how mortifying it was to have Mike witness my discovery of Tay's...disappearance. It was obvious to him that I knew nothing about it. And of course Madeline was ringside. That was fun for me, too. I mean, maybe Tay never slept with her, but he never made a complete jackass out of her, either. I guess she didn't have the requisite background to help him, and I did."

"Lucky you," Jane said.

Carol nodded dully.

Jane rose and took a cookie from the tray Carol had left untouched on the table. "Maybe we're being too hard on Tay. Neither one of us can imagine what it's like to lose your child like that, especially right after a spouse dies. His family was suddenly gone, in a twinkling. It's possible that he was just terrified that the Mayfields might succeed again on an appeal, so he decided to remove Alicia from contention while he had custody of her."

"He still used me, Jane," Carol said, wiping a tear from the corner of her eye. "He could call me just once, send me a cable, do something to let me know he's all right. But I'm not even worth that much consideration. It's obvious that all he wanted from the situation was the child. I was just a means to an end."

"Maybe something's happened to him."

"Oh, you mean that he was leading a secret life as a drug dealer and has been assassinated by a South American hit squad?"

"Well, you don't actually know what happened. It could be anything."

"I know how to draw a reasonable conclusion from the evidence, and so do you. Tay has taken his money and his child elsewhere and dumped me."

Jane swallowed the crumbs in her mouth and reached for another cookie. "All right," she said. "If that's true, then it's time you climbed out of this funk and got back into life. Jerry Ridge is having a Christmas party tomorrow night and you're coming with me."

Carol closed her eyes wearily. "Do I look like I'm ready for a Christmas party?"

"No, and that's why you have to come. There will be lots of men there. Jerry knows everybody. It will cheer you up."

"It will make me feel like the social reject that I am," Carol replied.

"Are you going to hole up in here and cry for the rest of your life?" Jane demanded.

"Yes."

"Carol, I've never seen you like this."

"I've never been like this. I feel like one of those people who go on talk shows to describe how they've been taken by a scam artist."

"But you wouldn't have to go on TV, Carol. According to you, everybody in the whole world already knows," Jane said, grinning mischievously.

"That isn't funny, Jane."

"I'm just trying to get you to lighten up a little. Are you planning to spend the holidays alone here staring at the four walls?"

"I'm hardly in the mood for a wassail bowl and chestnuts roasting on an open fire," Carol replied darkly.

"What does that mean?"

"It means that my aunt wants me to come to Massachusetts and John Spencer wants me to come to Strathmere to sign the papers for the sale of the house, but I'm staying here.''

''Is the house sold?''

''He says the agent has a contract with the buyer I chose, but there's a problem getting the mortgage or something.''

''You sound very interested.''

''I don't care, Jane. John can give the money from the sale to Gloria or to the deserving poor for all the difference it makes to me now.''

''Why don't you come to my mother's for Christmas?'' Jane asked. ''She'd love to see you.''

''Do you think I would add much to the festivities?''

''Oh, come on, you know my family. They'll all be too loaded to notice whether you're festive or not.''

Carol smiled weakly.

''Will you at least think about it?''

''I'll think about it, but I doubt I'll come.''

They looked up as Carol's mail thunked through the slot on her door.

''Should I get it?'' Jane asked, standing.

Carol shrugged. ''It's all bills.''

Jane shuffled over in her stockinged feet and lifted the stack of envelopes from the floor. She sifted through them quickly and then selected one, looking at Carol sharply.

''New Jersey State Board of Bar Examiners,'' she said, watching Carol's face.

Carol looked back at her but said nothing.

''Do you want to open it?'' Jane asked.

Carol bit her lip.

''I'll open it,'' Jane volunteered.

Carol nodded.

Jane slit the envelope with her thumbnail and extracted the single sheet of paper inside. She scanned the lines quickly and said, "You passed."

Carol exhaled, then nodded again.

"That's your reaction?" Jane said. "Passing the bar was the single goal of your life until . . ."

"Until I met Tay," Carol finished for her.

"And that's your only comment on this subject?" Jane said, waving the letter.

"Hip, hip, hooray," Carol muttered.

"Carol, you're depressed. You have to get out of here. Come to this party with me. If you hate it, we'll both ditch it."

"That's what you always say, and then when I want to go you have some excuse like you've ordered food, or just one more dance, or you're waiting to make some date before you leave."

Jane put her hand over her heart. "I promise. You have my word on it. I won't be able to have a good time thinking about you sitting here all alone like Scrooge with a bowl of gruel."

"What is gruel, anyway?"

"I don't know, in that old movie it looks like oatmeal. Listen, I'm going to go, I'm staying over at Julie's. I think I'll call my mother and ask her to check the mail and see if my letter came. I'll be back here at 7:00 p.m. tomorrow and you'd better be ready. Wear something fetching."

Carol groaned.

"Don't give me that," Jane said, putting on her coat. "You can be very fetching when you try, I've seen you." She wrapped her scarf around her neck and picked up her gloves. "How about that blue velvet dress you wore to the law review's Christmas party last year?"

"I think it has a stain on it."

"At least take it out and look at it, will you?"

"Okay."

Jane kissed her on the cheek. "I'll have Julie's car tomorrow, it's that beat-up red sedan, so look for it from the window."

Carol nodded. "Be careful on the way out, all the muggers have the Christmas spirit. Put your purse under your arm."

"Yes, Mother." Jane opened the door and slipped through it. Carol moved to the door and set the locks, then turned back to the empty room.

She knew that the blue velvet dress Jane had mentioned would not fit her, it would be too small in the waist.

Carol pulled out the top drawer in her desk and removed the pink box with the pregnancy test inside it.

Resolutely, she opened the top.

Jerry Ridge's party was in his loft on Great Jones Street. The hulks of abandoned factories being converted into yuppie apartment buildings surrounded Jane and Carol as they parked in the gravel-strewn lot across from Jerry's building. The night was cold and clear, and that part of the city seemed silent, abandoned like a gold rush town after a lode had been found elsewhere. But as they ascended in the open, wooden freight elevator to the fifth floor, the sounds of merrymaking drifted down the shaft.

"Is Jerry alone in this barn?" Carol asked.

"There are some artists and other bohemian types on the lower floors. I guess they're not home," Jane replied as they stepped out of the elevator and confronted a blank wall.

"To the left," Jane said.

"You've been here before?" Carol asked.

"Only once, but the route was indelibly imprinted on my mind. Just follow the noise."

They went down a narrow hall to a door that had a sheet of legal paper with Jerry's name on it tacked to the knocker. There was a red Christmas hat hanging on the knob. Jane knocked and the door was immediately pulled open by someone they didn't know.

"Come on in!" he said cheerily, then walked away.

Jane and Carol exchanged glances.

"We could be the vice squad," Carol said.

"I don't think Jerry's worried," Jane said dryly, taking off her coat. Carol followed suit, for the large room they entered was jammed with people and very warm. They were swallowed up immediately by the crowd.

The loft was vast, and Carol could tell that it was nicely furnished even with the press of humanity draped on and in every available space. She recognized Jerry, who had graduated two years before her class, and several other people from the law school, but the version of "Jingle Bell Rock" booming from the multiple speakers placed around the room precluded conversation. Jane went to get a drink, and Carol drifted gradually into a corner. When she acquired a pest who wouldn't get lost, she went into the kitchen and wound up serving a tray of canapes for the caterer. An hour later she was in the bathroom, throwing up into the sink.

She gradually realized that someone was tapping insistently on the door. She rose unsteadily to open it and saw Jane in the hall.

Jane groaned. "How did I know it would be you in here?" she said, sighing.

"I'm sick," Carol said.

Jane's exasperated gaze changed to one of concern and she came into the bathroom, shutting the door behind her.

"Something you ate?" Jane asked.

"Something I did. I'm pregnant."

Jane looked thunderstruck. "Tay?"

"No, Jane, old Mr. Jansen who picked up the trash in Strathmere. Of course it was Tay."

"Are you sure?"

"Yes. I took the test yesterday after you left."

"How long?"

"Over three months, I think. It must have happened the night of the storm. Neither one of us was exactly prepared, if you know what I mean. For a while I thought my periods were screwed up from stress, I've never been that regular anyway, but when my clothes started to get tight, I knew. And now, of course, I'm nauseated all the time. Forget morning sickness. I have it twenty-four hours a day."

Jane sat on the edge of the tub. "Wow."

"You said it."

"Have you thought about what you are going to do? Pretty soon it will be too late for—"

Carol held up her hand. "I've thought about it. I've suspected for a while, taking the test only confirmed my...condition."

Jane waited.

"I'm going to have the baby. I know that Tay was a slug, but I loved him. I still love him." She put her hand to her mouth. "Oh, no, I'm crying again."

Somebody pounded on the bathroom door and Jane shouted, "Get lost."

They heard irritated muttering, then the sound of departing feet.

"You should have told me, Carol," Jane said. "I never would have dragged you here tonight if I had known you were dealing with this as well as..."

"Tay's desertion?" Carol supplied, pulling a sheet of toilet paper off the roll and blowing her nose.

Jane nodded unhappily.

"Let's just leave, okay?" Carol said. "If I hear one more Christmas tune I'm going to punch somebody."

"I'll get our coats," Jane said, opening the bathroom door. As they filed out, a partygoer waiting nearby said, "What were you two doing in there?"

"Drop dead," Jane replied, and brushed past him.

He looked at Carol, who said, "Merry Christmas!" and followed her friend.

The two women talked quietly on the way back to Carol's apartment, mulling over Carol's plans. Jane declined Carol's invitation to come up for a while, so Carol stepped out into the snow and mounted the building's front steps by herself. By the time Carol unlocked the several locks on her door, she was more than weary, ready for bed.

She had left a kitchen light on, and as she walked through the hall by its shaded glow she saw a dark figure sitting in her armchair. Her heart stopped and she backed up, thinking in one split second of her life, her future, and her baby.

"It's all right, Carol," Tay said as he rose from the chair. "It's me."

Carol was speechless, staring as he came toward her and took shape in the dimly lit room.

"I still have my keys. You haven't changed the locks."

"Get out," Carol said hoarsely, the shock receding as she finally found her voice.

"Carol, wait a minute, let me explain..."

"Get out now, or I'm calling the police."

Tay stopped coming toward her, and she could see from his face that he was evaluating how to handle her. He was wearing a brown shearling jacket, unzipped to reveal a dark green crewneck sweater underneath.

She took off her own coat and reached for the phone.

"Carol, I know you're upset..." he began again.

"You don't know the half of it," she replied. "I'm dialing."

"You won't even hear me out?" he said.

"No. I don't care what you have to say, I've heard enough of your sad stories. It's ringing. Do you want to stay and listen to my official complaint?"

Tay was silent.

"I'm sure it won't be long before the Mayfields have a copy of the police report," Carol said nastily. "It should help them with their appeal, don't you think?"

"Would you give it to them?" Tay asked softly.

Carol didn't know how much longer she could maintain the pretense of control. "Just go," she said, not looking at him. "I don't want to talk to you."

He turned away, and Carol hung up the phone. She watched him walk out and then dropped into the chair he had vacated, too numb to cry.

She sat there for the rest of the night.

Eleven

Carol forced herself to go to work the next day, but she knew her diligence had been a mistake as soon as she saw the expression on Harold Smyth's face.

"Kirkland's in my office," he said to Carol. "He wants to speak to you."

Carol closed her eyes. "I'm so sorry to bring my personal life into your place of business," she said.

Smyth shook his head dismissively. "He came to see me for a professional reason, Carol. He's getting a restraining order against the Mayfields."

"A restraining order?" Carol said, stunned.

Smyth nodded, and Carol looked at him searchingly.

"Just listen to what he has to say," Smyth added. "I don't think you understand the situation. I know that from your point of view it looks like he walked out on you, but he didn't have a choice."

Carol didn't reply.

"You can use my office," Smyth said. "I'll make sure you aren't disturbed."

Carol walked past him down the gray-carpeted hall and entered the lush precinct of the senior partner's office with its Oriental rug, gilt framed pictures and immense cherrywood desk. Tay was standing by the picture window overlooking the street. He turned to face her as she came into the room.

It was Carol's first sight of him in daylight, and she noticed that he looked drawn, thinner. She could see him examining her, too, and she folded her arms over her waist protectively.

"I'm sorry I had to use Smyth to get you to see me," he said, taking his hands out of the pockets of his wool slacks. It was strange to see him in winter clothing, as it had been the previous night. He looked as he did in summer clothing: beautiful.

"I didn't expect blackmail to be beneath you," Carol answered, wishing that his eyes weren't quite so blue.

Tay sighed and said, "I'm just going to get this over with, because I can see that an elaborate lead-up isn't going to have any effect on you. I had to take Alicia into hiding because the Mayfields were going to snatch her."

Carol just looked at him.

"You don't believe me?" he said.

"You would have to come up with a hell of a story to cover your disappearing act," Carol said flatly.

His mouth tightened with anger. "Smyth is getting a restraining order to void their visitation rights and keep them two hundred yards away from Alicia at all times. Do you think a judge issues one of those against a politically connected millionaire and his lady wife without supporting evidence? You tell me, you're the lawyer."

Carol looked away from him.

"I know I was gone a long time, but it took me a while to convince the cops that I was right, I had to do it all long distance. They had to interview people ..."

"What people?"

"The housekeeper who warned me, for one. She slipped me a note when I came to the Mayfield house with the social worker to pick up Alicia."

"And what did it say?"

"That she had overheard conversations in which the Mayfields were planning to take Alicia from her school and then out of the country."

"Why would she tell you?" Carol said skeptically.

"She knew me from when I was married to Alice and she always thought the Mayfields had treated me badly. She thinks Alicia belongs with me."

Carol studied him, not sure of anything. "And you couldn't let me know where you were?"

"Of course not! They were trying to track me down, Carol, hoping to find us and take Alicia before I could convince the authorities that there really was a problem." He paused. "They had a private detective on you, too."

Carol's mouth opened, then closed firmly. "Come on," she said, her tone skeptical.

"It's true. Ask Smyth, it's in the housekeeper's deposition. You were watched in the hope that you would lead them to me." He spread his hands. "That's why I couldn't contact you."

Carol sat heavily in one of the guest chairs, trying to absorb what he was saying.

"I couldn't let them get Alicia, Carol. They have infinite resources, they could have taken her anywhere and I would never have seen her again."

"Where did you take her?" Carol whispered.

"I have an uncle the Mayfields don't know about, in the Blue Mountains. I just took Alicia and drove there, didn't stop along the way for food, brought extra gas in the trunk. Nobody saw me. I had a couple days' lead time because the Mayfields went on another vacation to help Regina to recover from the trauma of the hearing. By the time they came back for their first visitation, Alicia and I were gone."

"What did you tell Alicia?"

"That I was taking her on a trip to see a relative she had never met. When we stayed on and she began to ask questions, I told her we would go to my house as soon as we could. I kept it very vague, and kids adapt, but she still inquired a lot about her grandparents. She is fond of them." He paused. "She asked about you, too."

"You're not going to tell her about all this?"

"No. When she grows up and asks questions about the change in custody, I guess I'll have to tell her, but not before then."

"Where is she?" Carol asked.

"At my apartment with Mike and Madeline. Would you like to see her?"

Carol shook her head. He was not going to use her affection for his child to get her back.

Tay stared at Carol for a few seconds and then said in a resigned tone, "Are you finished with me, Carol? Just tell me if you are and I'll stop bothering you."

"I don't know," Carol replied quietly. "I have to think."

"Think about what? Either you love me or you don't."

"That's not the whole issue."

"What else is there?" Tay demanded.

"There are other considerations," Carol murmured.

"What the hell are you talking about?" he said, taking a step toward her.

Carol held up her hand, and he stopped.

"You can't just pop back into my life after a three-month absence during which I didn't know whether you were dead or alive and expect to pick up right where you left," Carol said.

"Why not?" Tay asked.

"My word, you are presumptuous," Carol said softly. "Do you think you are such a prize package that any woman would just sit around in limbo, knitting like Penelope, patiently waiting for you to return?"

"I think you would," he replied.

"Then I'm sorry you have such a low opinion of me," Carol said. She turned on her heel and left.

Tay stared at the closed door of the office long after she had gone.

Carol was swallowing a prenatal vitamin the size of a dirigible three nights later when the knocking commenced on her door.

"Carol, it's Tay. Let me in."

Carol put down her glass and was heading for the door when the locks on it started to turn one by one. She ran to drag an ottoman across the floor and prop it in front of the door.

"Go away, Tay!" she shouted.

"I'm coming in," he replied, and proceeded to do just that, throwing himself against the door so that the ottoman shot across the floor. Carol jumped back out of the way.

"Why didn't you tell me you were pregnant?" he demanded as the door sprang back. His face was taut with anger.

Carol stared at him. "How did you..." Then she stopped. "Jane," she said resignedly.

"That's right, and I'm glad she had the good sense to inform me that I'm going to be a father again." He slammed the door behind him and tore off his coat, tossing it onto a chair.

"It's none of your business. I'm handling it," Carol said shortly, turning away from him.

He grabbed her arm and forced her to face him. "You're carrying my child and it's none of my business?" he demanded incredulously.

"One third of the pregnancy is over, Tay, and I managed that just fine in your absence. I think I can get through the rest of it without your assistance."

"That isn't fair, Carol. I didn't know."

"You didn't ask. You knew how spontaneous that first night was, didn't it ever occur to you to wonder?"

"I guess I just thought the odds were against it."

"You didn't think at all. And neither did I. That's how people wind up in this situation."

His expression was odd, and she realized why when he said, "You're not considering..."

"No. I never did."

He swallowed hard. "Carol, you know how Alicia was taken away by Alice's parents, you know what that did to me. How could you even think of depriving me of another child?"

"Depriving you! Good heavens, will you listen to yourself? I didn't even know where you were!"

"You knew where I was when I came to see you here a couple of days ago. You knew where I was when we met in Smyth's office. Why didn't you say anything then?"

"You were telling me that surreal story about kidnapping plots and restraining orders and private detectives.

I was supposed to interrupt and blurt out, 'Oh, by the way, I'm pregnant'?''

"You weren't going to tell me, were you? You were just going to take off somewhere and have the baby."

"You're the expert on taking off, Tay. Not everyone is that selfish."

"Were you?" he insisted.

"I don't know, I don't know," Carol replied, putting her hand to her temples. "I haven't thought it through, this is just too much to handle all at once."

Tay watched as her face went blank suddenly and she bolted from the room. He was hovering when she returned a couple of minutes later, looking pale.

"What is it? What's the matter?" he asked anxiously.

"Nothing," she said, sinking into a chair. "I was just being sick. I have developed two new hobbies, vomiting and bursting out of my clothes. If you plan to stick around you'll have an opportunity to see both."

He went into the kitchen and got her a glass of water. "I plan to stick around," he said, handing her the drink.

Carol accepted it gratefully and drained half of it as he added, "Carol, I don't want to upset you, and I see that I'm doing just that."

She looked at him, unable to disagree.

"You know we have to talk," he said quietly. "Why don't you give me a call when you're ready? I can wait. When you feel able to discuss this, I'll come and see you. You know where I am and you can call me anytime."

Relief washed over Carol as she nodded mutely. Anything to get rid of him before she lost all dignity and threw herself into his arms.

"I'll go, then," he said, moving toward the door.

"Tay?"

He looked back at her.

"I'd like my keys," Carol said.

He reached into his pocket for a ring from which several keys dangled. He didn't look at her as he dropped it neatly on a table.

"Good night," he said softly, and left.

Carol closed her eyes and let her head fall back against the chair.

Tay paced around his apartment, skirting the Christmas tree he had put up for Alicia and the pile of presents for her on the floor. She had gone with Madeline to shop for a gift for him, and Tay was glad of the respite from explaining why she wouldn't be seeing Grandma and Grandpa over the holidays this year. He had always been proud of her intelligence, but bright kids asked a lot of questions, and it was a challenge to give answers that made sense to her without alarming her. Now with Alicia safely in hand he was free to worry about Carol, and how he was going to get her back.

He hadn't heard from her since his last visit to her place, and he was afraid that he wasn't going to hear from her in the future. The next night was Christmas Eve, and he couldn't bear the thought of not seeing her over the holidays. But she had gone several months without seeing him, when she was alone and pregnant, and now it seemed that she was unable to forgive him for that.

He sat suddenly and stared at the floor. He had certainly made a botch of everything. Getting Alicia back had cost him Carol.

The tweed pattern in the rug blurred in front of his eyes as he considered his life. Had he made the wrong decisions, taken the wrong turns? What else could he have done when he'd learned that the Mayfields were plan-

ning to snatch his child? He didn't have time to think
about anything except getting her out of harm's way, and
he had rashly assumed that Carol would understand. But
she had spent the time while he was gone feeling used and
deserted, and apparently that feeling couldn't be dispelled so easily.

The phone rang in the kitchen and he got up to answer it, thinking that it was Mike, who was supposed to
report in to him on the completion of a floor finishing
job. He lifted the receiver and said, "Yeah?" in a dis-
tracted tone.

"Tay, it's Carol."

He straightened and said alertly, "I'm glad you
called."

"Do you think you could drive up from Strathmere to
see me tomorrow night? I know there might be traffic
with the holiday and everything, but you're right in saying that we should get this resolved. . . ."

"I'll be there," Tay said quickly. "What time?"

"Is six okay? I'll get back from the office about five,
I'll leave the office party early, and that will give me some
time—"

"Six is fine," he said, interrupting her. "I'll see you
then." He hung up the phone before she could change her
mind, wondering if this visit would be their last. Or
would she give him another chance? He thought for a
moment, and then dialed New York information, putting his contingency plan into action.

Carol managed to escape the Christmas party fairly
quickly, dodging the partiers weaving in the halls as they
stumbled from office to office within the building, and
she emerged into the early winter darkness as a light snow
was falling. She decided to splurge on a cab and com-

peted for it with the last-minute shoppers trudging through the hardening slush, arms and bags loaded with packages. A charity worker dressed as Santa Claus rang his bell, its tinkle competing with the sound of a busker who was playing "God Rest Ye, Merry Gentlemen" on a harmonica. A group formed behind her as she flagged down a taxi, bolting in front of a man carrying an over-sized teddy bear. He gave her a dirty look as she climbed gratefully into the back seat.

Carol gave her address and was relieved when the cab-bie pulled away from the curb confidently, seemingly aware of the route to her destination. She sat back and watched the bright lights of Christmas in New York go by, glad that she was not among the throng of desperate consumers lured into one last retail outlet for a final orgy of spending. She thought about the coming evening with Tay, not sure whether she was feeling butterflies in her stomach or the first stirrings of movement from the baby. She looked up in surprise when the cabbie stopped in front of her building; even though they had moved through heavy evening traffic her reverie had made the trip seem short.

Carol emerged from the cab and gave the driver a hefty tip. He looked at the money and said, "Merry Christ-mas, Miss."

"Same to you," Carol replied, and slammed the door. She was preoccupied on her way up to her apartment, so she stopped short in alarm when she saw the light under her door. She tried the knob; it was unlocked. Her heart beating faster, she pushed it open and then gasped in surprise.

A fully decorated tree stood in her living room, sur-rounded by a pile of gifts. Tay stood next to the tree, wearing a welcoming but tentative smile.

"What is this?" Carol asked, dropping her purse and briefcase on a chair.

"What does it look like? Merry Christmas," Tay said.

"This breaking-and-entering act is getting a little old, isn't it? And how did you get in here, Tay? You gave me back my keys."

"Not before I had Mike copy them on his machine," Tay said sheepishly. "I already had a new set when I returned them to you."

"You are shameless," Carol said, sitting down to yank off her boots and then taking off her coat.

"I know."

"But the tree is beautiful. Thank you. I just didn't bother with one this year, it seemed so much work...."

"Everything's done, and dinner is in the oven."

"Don't tell me that you cooked something," Carol said, laughing as she pulled off her scarf.

"No. I got a take-out meal from Charlie O's and put it in there to keep warm."

"It seems you've thought of everything," Carol said.

He came over to her and took her hands in his. "Oh, you're cold," he said. "Come sit with me."

He led her to the sofa, and once they were settled on it he said, "There's one more thing I thought of."

"What's that?"

"I've never told you that I loved you, not in so many words, anyway."

"Yes, I know."

"I didn't really mean to avoid it for so long. I've thought it and known it, but I guess there was some part of me that felt those words should be reserved for Alice alone."

"And now?"

"She's dead, and we're alive. While I was away I realized that saying it or not doesn't mean a thing. I do love you, and you should hear it. I love you."

Carol felt her throat tighten with unshed tears.

"I asked you once before to marry me," Tay went on, "and you accepted. What's your verdict on that now? Are you still angry with me?"

Carol looked into his eyes and said, "I'm less angry than I was."

He sighed. "Do you think you will get over it?"

"I don't know. It may take a while."

"How long is 'a while'?" he asked, glancing at her burgeoning belly.

"I don't know, Tay, you can't expect me to forget all that's happened just because you suddenly show up and want to make amends. I asked you here tonight to tell you that I need time, that I won't be able to make a decision about this immediately."

"So the plan is to punish me?" he said resignedly.

"The plan is for me to think and think hard, something I wasn't doing a lot of before, and that resulted in my present circumstances. It strikes me that it's time for a new approach."

"What does that mean? You don't love me anymore?"

"I didn't say that. But I have a child to think about now."

"How could the child possibly be better off without its father?" he demanded.

"Don't badger me, Tay! I didn't hear from you for months, didn't know if you'd just skipped town or been murdered, and now you appear like a phantom and want to wrap up my future in five minutes. It's too much to deal with all at once. Can you understand that?"

"I understand that you hold all the cards and you're enjoying your position, letting me twist in the wind in retaliation for my supposed desertion."

"Supposed?" she said, arching one delicate brow.

"All right, all right," he said, rising and holding up his hands in surrender. "I guess you're entitled to get some of your own back, but I never thought that revenge was your style."

"This isn't revenge, Tay, I'm not that childish. All I can say is that if you want me, and you want our baby, you're going to have to wait."

"Wait for what?"

"For me to decide what to do."

"What decision do you have to make? Either you want me as a husband to you and a father to the child, or you don't."

"You may find this difficult to understand, Tay, but after the past several months of your unexplained absence the prospect of you as a husband has lost some of its luster."

He stared at her sullenly, not responding, while the oven's buzzer went off behind them.

Carol went into the kitchen and turned the oven off with a flick of her wrist.

"I appreciate the tree and everything else you've done. But it's going to take more than holiday decorations to make me forget what I went through while you were gone," Carol said to him as she returned to the living room.

"I had no choice but to do what I did," he said flatly. "If you can't understand that, I guess there's nothing more to say."

"I guess not."

He picked up his coat and shouldered into it, not looking at her.

"Jane called while I was here," he said quietly. "She said to tell you she passed the bar, too, she just received the letter. I didn't know you had gotten the results. Congratulations."

"Thank you."

Tay studied her face. "So how are we going to leave this? May I call you? Will you call me?"

"I'll call you when I have something to say."

"Which may be never?" he countered.

Carol was silent.

"I have rights as the baby's father," he said stiffly.

"Taking that attitude with me is not going to rack up any points in your favor," Carol replied crisply.

"Well, I'm sorry. I'm trying my best to win you back and make everything right and you're acting like I...betrayed you."

"You did. You betrayed my trust and my confidence and self-esteem. I've been slinking around like a whipped puppy since last September with everyone feeling sorry for me, the deluded Carol Lansing, dumped like trash by Tay Kirkland after she helped him get his child back."

"So that's what this is about? Your wounded pride?"

"It's about the four months I spent crying myself to sleep every night, wondering how I could have been so stupid, reliving every moment I spent with you and trying to find the lies and deceptions in what you had told me."

"I never lied to you! I didn't know I would have to disappear with Alicia until I found out the Mayfields were trying to snatch her!"

Carol shook her head, closing her eyes. "This is getting us nowhere, Tay. We're traveling in circles and I'm simply too tired to debate with you anymore. Please, just go home.''

He walked to the door and turned with his hand on the knob, looking back at her like Mickey Rooney leaving Boystown forever.

"I'm not giving up," he said. "I'll be around, you can count on it."

Carol watched as he closed the door behind him, then she slumped into a chair. The lights on the tree blurred into stars as her eyes filled with tears, and she reminded herself wearily to get up and fix the locks.

Then she fell asleep.

Tay was as good as his word. He showed up in her office at least once a week for the next couple of months, becoming a familiar figure and something of a running joke around the firm. On a blustery day at the end of February, Stella Winthrop, Harold Smyth's secretary, tapped on the side of Carol's cubicle and said archly, "He's here again. And this time he's brought his daughter with him."

Carol glanced at the clock. It was four-thirty and she had nothing pressing for the next half hour. She stood, saying, "Where is he?"

"In the reception area. You can take him into the conference room if you like. It's empty."

"All right." As Carol brushed past Stella, adjusting the hem of her overblouse, the older woman said, "Don't you think it's time you gave him a break? If I had someone that gorgeous chasing me all over New Jersey, and a baby on the way, I certainly wouldn't be playing hard to get."

Carol looked at Stella, at the iron-gray hair in a rigid beauty-parlor set. "You don't know the whole story, Stella," Carol said patiently.

"I know enough. I know that he's been coming back here every week despite the fact that you've been treating him like the dog's dinner. And if I may say so, that sweet little girl needs a mother—"

"Thank you, Stella," Carol said firmly, and went on down the hall to the lobby where Tay and Alicia were seated on a plaid sofa next to a potted plant.

Alicia bounded to her feet when she saw Carol, running to give her a hug.

"I've missed you!" she said, putting her hand on Carol's stomach. "Can I feel the baby?"

"I don't know if he's moving just now," Carol said, looking over the child's head at her father.

"Yes, he is!" Alicia said excitedly. "He's kicking!"

She stood, transfixed, for several seconds, then stepped back and looked up at Carol beseechingly.

"When are you going to marry my daddy?" she said.

Carol shot Tay a look, then said, "Alicia, why don't you go into the lounge just down the hall? There are some cookies and other snacks on the table and there's soda in the fridge. You can help yourself. Your father and I will be in the room just across the hall."

"Okay," the child said, and went skipping out of sight as Carol turned to face Tay.

"That was a dirty trick, bringing her here," Carol said.

"I thought it was time to haul out the big guns," Tay replied.

He was wearing a blue sweater that turned his eyes the color of cornflowers and his summer tan had faded to the point where she could see the windburn on his face.

Carol glanced away. Why did he always have to look so good? It didn't make resisting him any easier.

But then, was it really necessary to resist him any more?

"Let's go into the conference room," she said to him, and then led the way to the carpeted chamber with its oval oak table, leather chairs and book-lined shelves.

"Is this where all the big decisions are made?" he asked.

"Some of them."

They faced each other, several feet apart. Carol waited expectantly.

"I've come to give you something," he said.

"Is that so?"

He produced a folded contract from the back pocket of his jeans. Carol lifted the blue cover stapled to the front and saw that it was the contract of sale for the beach house in Strathmere.

"What are you doing with this?" she asked.

"Look at the name of the buyer," he said.

Carol looked at the purchaser's name typed into the space provided. "It's Hanover Enterprises, I already knew that," she replied, glancing up at him.

He held her gaze.

The light slowly began to dawn on Carol. "I see," she said slowly. "You're Hanover Enterprises, right?"

He nodded. "I formed a sub-corporation to buy the house. My mother's maiden name was Hanover."

"Did John Spencer know?" Carol asked.

"Yes."

"So you've been in this together?" Carol asked angrily.

"It wasn't a conspiracy to defraud you, Carol. I didn't want to see you lose the house and I knew if you were aware that I was buying it you might turn down the deal.''

Carol dropped the cover on the contract, saying nothing.

''Well?'' Tay prompted.

''I don't know what to say. Is this a bribe?''

''You can call it a peace offering.''

''Are we making peace?''

''Yes, we are,'' Tay said firmly. ''I think I've done sufficient penance for my sins and should be released from purgatory, and the baby is due in less than three months. If you marry me now and let me give my baby a name, if you aren't completely enchanted with me and my daughter by the time he is born I'll give you a divorce.''

''A divorce?''

''Yes.''

''So you're offering a trial marriage?''

''No, I'm offering a permanent one. I'm just telling you that I'll let you off the hook if you want to get out of it after you have the baby.''

Carol was silent for several seconds, and then said, ''You want me to marry you that badly?''

''I want you to marry me that badly.''

Carol sighed. ''Yes.''

He stared at her. ''Yes, what?''

''Yes, I'll marry you. And not on any trial basis, either. If I do it, I'm in it for keeps.''

''Do you mean that?'' he said softly.

''Yes. I can't take any more lectures from Stella Winthrop about what a beast I am to be spurning your suit.'' She bit her lip to keep from smiling. ''And I miss you. And Alicia. I've given it a lot of thought, and I want us to be a family.''

He covered the distance between them in one stride and embraced her tightly. At the same moment Alicia entered the room, carrying a bag of potato chips.

"Carol and I are getting married," her father announced.

"Hurray!" the child replied, and threw her chips into the air.

Tay stepped back from Carol, his eyes shining. "Let's get out of here and celebrate," he said.

The three of them left the conference room hand in hand.

*   *   *   *   *

COMING NEXT MONTH

Yo amo novelas con corazón!

Starting this March, Harlequin opens up to a whole new world of readers with two new romance lines in SPANISH!

Harlequin Deseo
- passionate, sensual and exciting stories

Harlequin Bianca
- romances that are fun, fresh and very contemporary

With four titles a month, each line will offer the same wonderfully romantic stories that you've come to love—now available in Spanish.

Look for them at selected retail outlets.

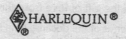 HARLEQUIN®

SPANT

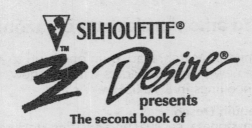

SILHOUETTE®

Desire®

presents

The second book of

SONS AND *Lovers*

AVAILABLE FEBRUARY 1996

REESE: THE UNTAMED
by Susan Connell (SD #981)

Reese Marchand was a scandalous playboy with an even more scandalous secret—and sexy Beth Langdon was determined to uncover it!

SONS AND *Lovers* : Three brothers denied a father's name, but granted the gift of love from three special women.

"For the best miniseries of the decade, tune into SONS AND LOVERS, a magnificent trilogy created by three of romance's most gifted talents."

—Harriet Klausner
Affaire de Coeur

Coming in March:

RIDGE: THE AVENGER—Leanne Banks (3/96)

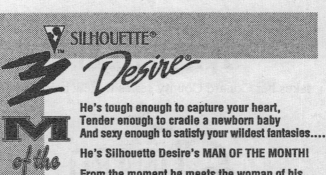

Bestselling author

RACHEL LEE

takes her Conard County series to new heights with

A CONARD COUNTY Reckoning

This March, Rachel Lee brings readers a brand-new, longer-length, out-of-series title featuring the characters from her successful Conard County miniseries.

Janet Tate and Abel Pierce have both been betrayed and carry deep, bitter memories. Brought together by great passion, they must learn to trust again.

"Conard County is a wonderful place to visit! Rachel Lee has crafted warm, enchanting stories. These are wonderful books to curl up with and read. I highly recommend them."
—*New York Times* bestselling author
Heather Graham Pozzessere

Available in March, wherever Silhouette books are sold.

"Motherhood is full of love, laughter and sweet surprises. Silhouette's collection is every bit as much fun!"
—Bestselling author **Ann Major**

This May, treat yourself to...

WANTED:
MOTHER

Silhouette's annual tribute to motherhood takes a new twist in '96 as three sexy single men prepare for fatherhood—and saying "I Do!" This collection makes the perfect gift, not just for moms but for all romance fiction lovers! Written by these captivating authors:

Annette Broadrick
Ginna Gray
Raye Morgan

"The Mother's Day anthology from Silhouette is the highlight of any romance lover's spring!"
—Award-winning author **Dallas Schulze**

MD96